THE STRANGE CASE
OF MR PELHAM

edited and with an introduction by
Nick Smith

First published in the UK by Methuen & Co 1957

This edition first published by B7 Media 2021
Unit 2, Whitegates, Berries Road, Cookham, Berkshire, SL6 9SD

Hardback ISBN: 978-1-914169-32-8
Paperback ISBN: 978-1-914169-33-5
E-book ISBN: 978-1-914169-34-2

www.B7media.com

This edition of
The Strange Case of Mr Pelham
is dedicated to
Kate Armstrong Willis,
Anthony Armstrong's granddaughter

By the same author

My Friend Seraphin
Prangmere Mess
Warriors at War
Warriors at Ease
Warriors Still at Ease
Selected Warriors
Easy Warriors
Livestock in the Barrack
Captain Bayonet and Other Warriors Paraded: A Military Omnibus
Thoughts on Things
Britisher on Broadway
While You Wait
Two Legs and Four
How to do it
Percival and I
Percival at Play
Apple and Percival
Me and Frances
The After-Breakfast Book
Nothing to do with the War

Spies in Amber
He Was Found in the Road
No Higher Mountain
The Trail of Fear
The Secret Trail
The Trail of the Lotto
The Poison Trail
The Trail of the Black King
Ten Minute Alibi (with Herbert Shaw)

Patrick, Undergraduate
Patrick Engaged
Patrick Helps
No Dragon: No Damsel

Yesterdailies
The Prince who Hiccupped — Fairy Tales for Grown-ups
The Naughty Princess — Fairy Tales for Grown-ups
Taxi!

Cottage into House
We Like the Country
Village at War
We Keep Going
The Year at Margaret's

By ANTHONY ARMSTRONG and RAFF
Pilot Officer Prune's Progress

By RAFF and ANTHONY ARMSTRONG
Plonk's Party of the A.T.C.
Nice Types
More Nice Types
Goodbye, Nice types

Introduction

There can be little doubt that Anthony Armstrong would have whole-heartedly approved of this reissue of his classic 1950s thriller The Strange Case of Mr. Pelham. This conclusion can only be drawn indirectly, but there exist the sort of clues that Armstrong himself would have liked, if you know where to look for them.

Writing from his country cottage Margarets, deep in a leafy corner of Hampshire, Armstrong—a man who produced so many words that you can only deduce that he loved the process of committing them to paper—is apologising to one of his readers over the lack of availability of his earlier books. In a surprisingly long note to a stranger, he confides in Mrs Hislaw that he shares her sense of an injustice perpetrated. "I am sorry," he types on an old manual typewriter early one September at some point in the 1960s, "but nothing can be done about the books, except keep an eye open for them at second-hand bookshops. They have been out of print for some years now and I am constantly getting letters—to my annoyance, for the publishers would not reprint them – telling me there was no longer a demand. My daughter has picked up *Village at War* and *We Keep Going* on a second-hand bookstall at Cambridge, but those are the only spares even I have!"

What's interesting about this unpublished letter, signed in his customary turquoise ink, is not so much that Armstrong is referring to his quintet of 'Country House' memoirs that were so popular during the Second World War and the decade that followed. Rather that he mentions towards the end that, as he is now a presenter on a national television gardening show, he had assumed that this would lend his out-of-print works the kind of sympathetic magic that might get the presses rolling again. His letter finished on a plaintive note, wondering if publishers will ever again be interested in his earlier books. Sixty-four years after it first appeared in our bookshops in 1957, and nearly half a century after its author's death, *The Strange Case of Mr. Pelham* has finally caught a publisher's eye. With the publication of this edition of Pelham, we have the only 21st century reissue of this superb British tale of suspense, welcomed by one of today's finest spy thriller writers Mick Herron, who expresses a sentiment that will be echoed by aficionados of the genre: "It's a pleasure to see Anthony Armstrong's classic back in print, ready to unnerve a new generation of readers with its eerie tale of fractured identity."

While it is tempting to construct from Armstrong's letter to Mrs Hislaw the picture of a struggling author who'd never quite fulfilled his potential, nothing could be further from the truth.

Although we can't be exactly sure of when he wrote his characteristically charming note, the evidence points to it post-dating the publication of *The Strange Case of Mr. Pelham*. Arguably his most successful novel, it was published on both sides of the Atlantic, translated into several languages, dramatised for radio broadcast and committed to celluloid for both television and the silver screen. The fact that the cover design of the British first edition of Pelham includes a superb duotone illustration commissioned from a hugely popular artist of the day, Albany Wiseman, suggests that the publisher Methuen & Co took the book's production and reputation seriously enough to invest real money in it.

Although it has fallen into a deep and, some would say, unjustified obscurity, the name Anthony Armstrong was once one to be reckoned with. Although it's hard to be certain how many books he wrote in a career spanning six decades, once the thrillers, romances, comedies of manners, war memoirs, country house reminiscences, plays, collections of journalism, children's books and anthologies are taken into account, it's a safe bet that he saw to press more than a hundred, and that untangling the oeuvre would present a serious challenge to a bibliographer. Despite being such a prolific author, outside specialist book collecting circles, these days Armstrong is only really remembered for his novel *The Strange Case of Mr. Pelham* (that started out as a short story), and perhaps his play *Ten Minute Alibi* (that ended up as a novel). That these works have remained in the public eye at all is largely due to the fact that they were both made into classic British crime films. *Ten Minute Alibi* was produced in 1935 at Beaconsfield Studios (now the National film and Television School), while Pelham, after a long and complex history of radio and television productions (in which the legendary filmmaker Alfred Hitchcock plays a significant part), went on to become the 1970 psychological thriller *The Man Who Haunted Himself*, starring Roger Moore, fresh off the back of the success of *The Saint*.

While Moore was to scale even greater heights playing the role of secret agent James Bond in seven of the 007 movies, in his memoir – My Word is My Bond – he says that he rated Harold Pelham as his apex character performance: "it was a film I actually got to act in, rather than just being all white teeth and flippant and heroic." Moore recalls how he immersed himself in the narrative to produce an intense and layered role. He seized Pelham with gusto, portraying his psychological deterioration as his reputation and family life are dismantled by outside forces. As one commenter says: "Moore expertly worked the source material and screenplay to show the horror of a decent, successful family man reduced to insanity as he's stalked by an unexplained doppelgänger, indulging in the excesses of London society in the late 1960s."

The Strange Case of Mr. Pelham is Armstrong's own novelisation of a short story dating back to the 1930s, in which the protagonist is an innocuous, conventional, traditionalist English bachelor, who acquires a doppelgänger with an opposite personality and a sinister agenda. Opening in Monte Carlo, the story is told through the eyes of a young couple exploring a casino, where they learn of a mysterious gambler by the name of Pelham. Intrigued by both Pelham and his glamorous companion, they delve into the stranger's past, only to discover that not long before he had been a different man. In the manner of the suspense thriller of yesteryear, Armstrong's narrative deftly unfolds as Pelham becomes aware of a mystery 'double' taking advantage of his socially distant life. As this almost paranormal figure makes its influence more known, a creeping terror begins to infect Pelham, whose inconspicuous existence is thrown out of equilibrium. A series of apparent coincidences and mistaken identities initially creates moments of confusion and mild levity, only to gradually accelerate into something more sinister, causing Pelham to spiral into a psychological crisis as his doppelgänger takes control.

While most contemporary reviews tended to politely agree that The Strange Case of Mr. Pelham was "a lightly amusing tale of suspense and terror," perhaps the most perceptive analysis came from one critic—his name now lost to history—who read the tale as "an extraordinarily irritating piece of cleverness." Although his letter to Mrs Hislaw may not have overbrimmed with confidence about the future of his series of memoirs recounting the bucolic idyll of family life at Margarets, Armstrong was much more optimistic about the path ahead for a story that was to stay with him in one form or another for much of the second half of his career.

In his unpublished four-volume autobiography Funny Side Up, he goes into some detail about the trajectory of his most famous creation:

"As a matter of interest that original short story, The Strange Case of Mr. Pelham, had a most profitable and varied career. It was first published in the American magazine Esquire in 1940, was next broadcast over there as a playlet in 1941, done three times on BBC Radio in 1946, and later twice on TV, published over here in Britannia and then in two other magazines, turned into a film script (as stated above), published again in America and three times on the continent. In 1955 it was done yet again on both BBC and US TV, and also in Australia and New Zealand, after which I turned it into a full-length novel which was published here and in New York and finally in Italy. Not bad for one small short story. It'll probably bob up again somewhere yet."

Nick Smith
Swansea
December 2020.

A note on the text:

This edition of The Strange Case of Mr. Pelham is based on the text of the first UK trade edition published by Methuen & Co in 1957. While every reasonable care has been taken to ensure the accuracy of the original text, the opportunity has been taken to silently correct the more obvious typographical errors of punctuation and spelling that are inevitably present in any first edition.

THE STRANGE CASE OF MR PELHAM

by
Anthony Armstrong

1

If a chilly little wind had not started to rustle in from the east over Monte Carlo harbour that late autumn evening, David and Joanna Lightfoot would probably never have met Mr Pelham—and their life would have followed a far different and far happier course. But, gradually, the still reflections of the harbour lights and the moon became increasingly ruffled into trembling cascades of ruby and emerald and pearl, till at last Joanna said, "Brr!" and involuntarily shivered. At once her young husband took her arm, and instead of continuing their proposed walk round the humped headland of Monaco old town, steered her solicitously back towards Monte Carlo, till, as if by accident, they found themselves outside the Casino. Here David appeared to be struck with a sudden idea.

"I say, Jo darling, what about going in and having a crack at the tables?"

"Didn't we say we weren't going to tonight?"

"I know. But I've all at once got a feeling that my luck's in."

Joanna laughed, seeing through him, tolerant of his speciousness. "We agreed that tonight we'd be firm, and just walk round the rock and look at the lights on the water and the moon and..."

"But then it got too chilly and that's part of my hunch. See! Fate absolutely drove us away from the lights on the water straight to the door of the Casino." He grinned persuasively. "For what purpose? Why, to win a packet."

"Darling, what are you going to use for money? You *know* we've only got just enough to last us till we go home on Friday."

"We could use that."

"Heavens! Suppose we lose?"

"Then we'll have to leave here tomorrow. On the other hand..."

1

"But I don't want to go back before we planned. It's three whole days, and I love this place. I'd like to stay even longer. Oh, damn the currency restrictions!"

"They're better than they were."

"And the absurd thing is we can easily afford to stay well beyond Friday, if only…"

"If only the money wasn't at home; I know. Compulsory paupers—that's the English abroad."

"Well, I think it's all idiotic. Why on earth can't the Government…"

"Come off it, Jo! I know words and music by heart. Look here! Shall we have a gamble?"

"I thought that's what all the argument was about."

"No, I mean a real one." He had taken his wallet from his pocket and pulled out the notes it contained. "Listen! We've got our return tickets and two thousand for journey money tucked safely away in our room, haven't we?"

"Yes, and who made you do that"

"Well, here's *this* for the hotel bill to date: I checked with them this afternoon." He counted out some notes. "Now, let's see, dinner was two thousand two hundred. Then there's our room tonight, and tomorrow's breakfast." He calculated further, added some more notes and held up the little wad. "This lot will take care of our hotel up to midday tomorrow. And *this*"—he held up the rest—"is what's over and is to try our luck with tonight."

"But David! That…"

"Listen, darling! Here's the gamble I mean. You just said you'd like to stay longer; very well then, take a sporting chance on it. Either we leave tomorrow, or we turn this little packet into staying on here for—well, it depends on how much we win."

Joanna's eyes suddenly sparkled. All at once she was attracted by the idea. "Maybe you have got something, darling."

"I have. Don't you see we're staking at most three days against possibly six, nine, a fortnight—who knows? And, quite honestly, I do have the feeling that luck's with me tonight."

Joanna hesitated a moment longer. Then she said: "O.K. Let's. But I'm going to keep the hotel money just in case you decide on another gamble and we stay on that fortnight in a prison cell." She took the first wad of notes from him and put it firmly in her bag. "Only over my dead body."

David was counting the other roll. "Roughly about fifteen thousand," he said. "We ought to do something with that."

"I hope it's a nice day for travelling tomorrow," said Joanna resignedly. "Well, come on in."

The large hall with the roulette tables was crowded, every chair taken, and people standing behind betting over the shoulders of those seated.

"No places," murmured Joanna, when David had changed their notes into plaques and they had walked round the room.

"Bother! My hunch says I've *got* to gamble sitting down tonight. Besides, when my money's on the table in front of me I can see how much I'm making."

"Your hunch certainly seems on the job," replied Joanna lightly, though she was really as excited as he was. "Did it remind you to order the truck to cart the stuff away afterwards? Well, let's wait at this table here. I'm sure that man with the purple dinner-jacket is going bust soon."

"No, that's not the table for tonight." He took her arm and steered her to one on the far side of the room. "Yes," he announced solemnly, as if deciding on a purchase in a shop, "yes, this is ours, I think."

"Good old hunch! *He* knows! Come on then! We'll get behind those two old ladies."

They moved over and waited, standing close behind the line of seated gamblers.

"That chap at the far end, on the right of the croupier, is doing well," remarked Joanna after a while. "Look at that pile in front of him and he's just won some more."

"Ah, but you don't know how much he's lost earlier on."

"True. Or how much he had to start with."

"More than us, I'll bet."

"He's won again," said Joanna, a few minutes later.

David looked along to the end. "His girlfriend's losing it for him, though. The piece with all the jewellery. He's just passed her a couple of ten-thousands."

3

While his wife continued to watch the lucky gambler, David studied the girl. She was young, beautifully dressed, had coppery-red hair and seemed from that distance extremely attractive. He felt a sudden urge to move over to that half of the table and get a closer look, but it was more crowded and he did not wish to miss his chance of a seat.

"*Rien ne va plus*," intoned the croupier, as the little ball clattered round on its money-making, money-losing course. A moment later it was trapped to circling immobility and he announced loudly, with the hint of satisfaction peculiar to the breed on such occasions: "*Le Zéro!*"

A little buzz broke out round the table, and in a few minutes, Joanna again turned to her husband.

"There's something funny about that man, David. Well, I don't really mean funny. But he's betting very high and winning quite a lot and behaving as to the manner born and... There! See!"

At that moment, with a pleasant yet somehow sardonic little smile, the man, who had won again on the next throw, casually pushed a high-denomination plaque towards the croupier at his end of the table with a "*Pour la service!*"

"These croupiers cut it pretty fat, don't they? Whacking tips when someone brings off a killing, and don't have to give it back if the chap loses... But what's funny about him? Most people tip the..."

"The—the poise," Joanna explained, "yet he looks like a small-town businessman."

"Oh, I see what you mean. Yes, he is frightfully ordinary to look at."

"Do you think he's an absconding bank clerk from Surbiton, having a good old fling before the police catch up with him?"

"Not likely. All that man-of-the-world stuff couldn't have been acquired by a bank clerk in years. Nor by a retired Army major, for that's what he looks like too. But he's certainly a puzzle. Those evening clothes didn't come from Surbiton."

"The girl must cost a bit too. I wouldn't mind betting that's a Dior, and her jewellery isn't Woolworth exactly. Still, I expect she's worth every penny of it, don't you think?" she added mischievously.

"She doesn't interest me," returned her husband loftily, and not very truthfully.

"I see. Someone has to twist your arm first." She scrutinised the girl again. "She doesn't fit in with him either. Much too much of a glamour-puss to go with that little clipped moustache and round face and slightly worried look, and—well, general insignificance. I can't see his eyes from here but I wouldn't be surprised if they were like a spaniel's—gooey and pleading, you know. I *wonder* what he is!"

"Personally, I can't put it higher than manager of an insurance office."

"Then he must have managed to insure quite a lot of people all living to a hundred... Oh, look! He's lost for once. I was..."

Her left arm was suddenly taken in a friendly grasp just above the elbow. Turning, she saw Fred Dyson, a holiday-made acquaintance staying at the same hotel. His other hand was similarly holding her husband.

"Hullo, you two! Didn't you say this morning you were giving up gambling hells? You've got to last till Friday, haven't you?"

"No. David's decided we're going to last for another ten days, or only till tomorrow."

"It's going to be ten days, Fred. There's luck at this table tonight. We've been watching a fellow... Oh, perhaps *you'd* like a guess. What do you put that chap down there as? Bank clerk, insurance, retired Army?"

"Which one? Oh, that's Mr Pelham! J. M. Pelham."

"You know him?"

"Well, met him once briefly. But I know an acquaintance of his fairly well, a Captain Masters who spends a lot of time out here, and he took me along to a party Pelham threw two nights ago, after he'd made a killing at baccarat." He chuckled. "He's no bank clerk or insurance type though. He's in business, and..."

"Ah, I said a small-town businessman right at the start," exclaimed Joanna with satisfaction.

"Small-town? Not on your life. He's big. An importing and exporting firm in London. Masters gave me some of the lowdown on him."

"What does he import and export?"

"All sorts of things; I haven't a clue. But whatever they are he does darn' well out of it; I imagine he's pretty wide."

"Wide?"

5

"Clever, darling, he means. Even tricky, eh, Fred?"

"Yes, I gather it's not what he imports and exports, but the way he does it."

"How? Oh, smuggling?" Joanna was highly intrigued. "Do you mean he's a kind of crook?"

"Quiet, Jo!" David looked quite nervous. "I don't know what the libel laws in France are, but don't let's find out the hard way!"

"I see." She lowered her voice. "But I'm *interested*."

"What I mean, Joanna, is that—except one thing that this Captain Masters hinted at, and that probably *was* a libel—there's never been any breath of…"

"Scandal?"

"No, no. It's hard to explain, but if you're in business and you're hedged round with silly regulations and officious Customs officers and declarations in quadruplicate and so forth, you've got to be smart if you're not to go under. And he's as clever as a hatful of monkeys— that's Master's description, by the way."

"Well!" ejaculated David, much impressed. "I'd never have believed that that class of chap could look so plain ordinary."

"They don't. I should say he's unique in that respect. But, just occasionally, his eyes give him away. They're—they're—well, they sort of change."

"Nothing wrong with his eyesight when it comes to picking a girl," remarked David appreciatively. "She's a smasher. Though distance may be lending enchantment."

"Not on your life. She's unique in a way too. I've only talked to her once, at that party the other night, but—oh boy!" He broke off with a laugh. "Seriously though, they're the queerest pair I've ever met."

"Who is she?"

"His secretary, I think. Anyway she goes everywhere with him, and…"

Joanna here interrupted. A fragment of their earlier conversation which had intrigued her at the time suddenly came back to her mind. "I say, Fred! You said just now something about Captain Masters hinting at one thing about Mr Pelham's business…"

"It wasn't to do with his business."

"Then it sounds even more interesting. Tell me!"

"I said it was probably a libel, so I'd better not…"

"Oh but please! I want to know."

"It was only some kind of rumour. Happened last year. Something about a party on his yacht with some young people, and drugs and things. One girl was quite ill and the story was he and his fancy piece there had been teaching the youngsters to experiment with drugs. His parties are pretty wild anyway, but I expect this was only a bit of spicy embroidery. The girl had merely drunk more than she could take—and you know what rumours are. And, honestly, Joanna, I don't think we ought to pull him to pieces like this. He's just a clever businessman and cleverness, in business, covers a lot of…"

"But there must have been…"

"Has he partners in his firm?" asked David, catching a mute appeal for help from the other.

"Honestly, I haven't an idea. I…" He broke off and waved to a lean spare man with an aquiline nose and a heavy moustache who had come up behind the players on the far side of the table. "But there's the very chap for you, if you're both so interested—Masters himself." He beckoned and the tall man smiled and nodded and made his way round to them.

"Hullo, Dyson!" He smiled at the other two, anticipating the introduction.

"Hullo there! May I introduce you to Mrs Lightfoot—Captain Masters—and her husband David Lightfoot!"

"Pleasure. Seen you about with Dyson once or twice. Havin' luck?"

"We haven't played yet."

"They're far too interested in Mr Pelham there. Fairly badgering me about him and I only know just the few things you mentioned the other night."

"Oh, Jim Pelham? Strange type, isn't he?" laughed Masters. "The difference between his external appearance and…"

"Yes, that's what intrigued us in the first place," David cut in.

"They were asking just now if he had business partners."

"Lord no! He's very much on his own. Doubt if any partner could keep up with him. Smart as a whistle. Pelham Lake and Co. is his firm,

7

but Lake was only a figurehead and, anyway, died years ago, so he's had it for a long while. Funny thing is, though, that it was an awful stick-in-the-mud concern, conservative and unenterprising, y'know, up till about a year back when he suddenly launched out in a big way. Brought off some most amazin' coups, I'm told, all inside of three months."

"Maybe," suggested Fred Dyson, "he suddenly realised all he was missing in life, and decided to pull his socks up, make money and have fun."

"Possibly. Though of course…"

"You mean," interrupted Joanna, "that before the time he pulled his socks up, as Fred says, he was just like—well, like what he still looks."

"Imagine so. But what I was goin' to say was, just about that time he had rather a shock, which may have had quite a bit to do with it."

"What? Something like a bang on the head," asked David, "which suddenly put the old brain into top gear?"

"No. Mental shock. He had a nasty, unnervin' experience. A strange case altogether."

2

Mr James Pelham had a quiet pleasant flat on the fourth floor of Clitheroe Court, Maida Vale, London, N.W. Here he lived a quiet and pleasant bachelor life, looked after by his manservant Rogerson. Rogerson had originally come to him, on the unexpected death of his predecessor, for a month's trial only, Mr Pelham having explained that, though he had simple tastes and was not difficult to please, he did insist on the flat being run in smooth and orderly fashion, his clothes properly cared for, meals regular and well cooked, and the whole place kept neat and tidy; and that it would be better, therefore, for both of them to find out whether they would suit one another, since Mr Pelham was looking for someone permanent. To this Rogerson had rather unexpectedly replied that he was not difficult to please either, having no marked ambitions other than for a quiet orderly life in a simply-run gentleman's establishment; while as for cooking and general neatness, his three previous employers—four, seven, and three years respectively—had unanimously praised the former, and only one of them had found fault on the latter score. "And that, sir, if I may venture the opinion, was unfortunately due to the fact that he was himself of an extremely untidy disposition."

Mr Pelham had taken to him right away for his answer, and before the month was half over had expressed complete satisfaction and definitely engaged him for as long as he cared to stay.

Rogerson, apparently equally satisfied, had now been with him—let's see, thought Mr Pelham, shaving at his hand-basin in the fresh sunlight of an early May morning—just on four years. No, it was five: five years exactly in about a week. Every time the anniversary came round, Mr Pelham formally wished Rogerson many happy returns and presented him with a five-pound note, invariably adding whimsically that he wondered how much longer they'd continue to put up with one another. He had a note of the precise date in his pocket diary, into which each 1st

9

January he transferred from the previous year such anniversaries as he wished to remember. Being a bachelor with no near relatives, the majority of these were of the same benevolently paternal order, typical of Mr Pelham's kindly nature—his secretary's birthday, the wedding day of her predecessor, the christening of a schoolgirl god-daughter, the birthday of the small son of the club billiard-marker of whom, Mr Pelham, a regular player, saw a good deal, and similar dates, the suitable recognition of which, he found, gave so much pleasure.

Five years, thought Mr Pelham, was quite a long time. He stopped shaving temporarily to consider an idea that had come to him. Why not signalise it with something a little more personal than the usual gift of money? Or rather, in addition to it: after all, five years, half a decade, was a definite landmark. A silver cigarette-case now would be nice; with the date and Rogerson's name inscribed on it. Accompanied, of course, by a card reading "To Rogerson from J. M. Pelham. A memento of five happy years", or something like that. And—for Mr Pelham was fond of what he called "pleasant little quips"—"The first five years are the hardest".

Rogerson would laugh at that, or rather permit himself a deferentially approving smile, thought Mr Pelham, as he resumed his shave, guiding the razor carefully round his neat little moustache. Ah well, he was a lucky man to have such a good servant who ordered his life so smoothly. And Rogerson was lucky too: not all servants had considerate masters... He frowned severely at himself in the mirror: he mustn't take personal credit like that. Being considerate was only part of a kindly disposition and that was a gift of nature, not his own doing.

He finished shaving, had his bath, dressed in his usual neat dark business suit and went down the short passage from the bedroom to the hall. Here he paused to tap the barometer, then hurried along another short passage which led to the small dining-room opposite the kitchen.

About an hour later he was in the Bakerloo tube, happily unfolding his paper. It was a lovely morning and he had enjoyed his walk from the flat to Warwick Avenue tube station. On wet days he took a taxi, short though the distance was, and in the evenings nearly always taxied all the way home from his office in Bedford Street, Strand. Indeed, he was an inveterate taxi user, for he hated buses and only just tolerated the tube, when going to work in the mornings, because it gave him nice time to read his paper. He stoutly maintained that taxis were cheaper and less worry than a private car, driving which in London was almost impossible anyway, and that the added comfort over buses and tubes in the rush hour was well worth the money. It was quite a little hobbyhorse of his and his friends at the Savernake Club pulled his leg about it: "Old Pell on the Economic Advantages of the Taximeter Cab!" He was frequently referred to as "old Pell", though he was only forty: it was a blend of affection and recognition of his orderly bachelor habits.

From Trafalgar Square station, Pelham walked a short distance along the Strand till he came to a jeweller's where he called in to choose the cigarette-case for Rogerson. Before definitely ordering it, he insisted on an assurance that they would have it ready inscribed by the following Monday evening—he had verified from his diary that next Tuesday was the great day—and then continued along the Strand till he came to Bedford Street.

About a hundred yards up on the left he arrived at No. 13A, walked up to the first floor, opened the door marked "Pelham Lake & Co. Mr James M. Pelham. Private" and entered his personal office where he hung his hat and neatly rolled umbrella on a hook. He always carried this latter, rain or fine, for the simple reason that he liked hailing taxis with it. Rather than shout or wave he would stand in a dignified manner on the kerb with umbrella raised till a cab drew up.

Next, he put his head through the door to the main office and said his usual friendly good morning to the head clerk, old Danvers, and the rest of the staff. Then he settled himself comfortably at his desk, arranged the objects on it a little more precisely, lit a cigarette and pressed the desk-bell for his secretary.

In a moment she came in from her own small office adjacent, carrying shorthand pad, pencil and the morning's mail which she placed in front of him as she greeted him cheerfully.

Lily Clement was young, pretty, and efficient with very expressive deep-blue eyes, a lovely complexion, rather ordinary brown hair, and a ripely generous full-lipped mouth. She thought a lot of her employer, appreciating his invariable kindness and consideration, but at times she found herself wishing he could be a little more forceful in his business methods. Like many of her sex she admired masculine push and authority, the go-getting spirit.

"Good morning, Miss Clement," replied Pelham. "Isn't it a lovely spring day?" He glanced cursorily at the letters. "Anything urgent?"

"There's this, Mr Pelham." She proffered a folder she had been keeping back.

"Ah, the Manson folder." Pelham recognised it with distaste. "Yes, I'll go into it today sometime," he went on, but put it under some other documents in a tray.

"You did that with it yesterday: you're really being terribly naughty," the girl scolded, and instantly wondered whether she hadn't been a little too familiar. But Pelham, now absorbed in one of the letters, hadn't heard, which was just as well, she felt, if she had been. Somehow or other, for all their eight months' association, they had never reached that sense of close camaraderie, of mutual understanding which so often exists between employer and confidential secretary and which has incidentally also been often known to cause suspicion in the home circle. Lily Clement thought this a great pity—particularly as Mr Pelham had no home circle where that sort of suspicion could be caused. Without exactly dramatizing life or herself, she liked every human relationship whatever it might be—brother and sister, lover and mistress, uncle and niece, boyfriend and girl, employer and secretary—to conform to her conception of its proper pattern.

But though Mr Pelham was always friendliness itself, there was a certain shyness and formality about him which was not to her mind the correct attitude. Or rather—she giggled inwardly—the incorrect one. She felt that at some time in the last months he should have suggested taking her out to dinner or a theatre with perhaps a hint of inner meaning, and she'd have been able to refuse—kindly but firmly, so that he'd realise clearly the sort of girl she was; and then they could settle down in their recognised and fully understood roles, which yet at times might provide interesting moments. Beyond chocolates and flowers, however, he'd never made a single even slightly equivocal gesture—and those had been on her birthday and at Christmas, which wasn't at all the same thing. She sighed, for she was really very fond of Mr Pelham, would have liked to be on more intimate—no, not quite the right word, again she giggled inside herself—more customary terms.

"Anything worrying you?" Pelham had looked up at the sigh, suddenly solicitous.

"Dear me, no," she smiled. As if she could tell him.

"That's good. But honestly, Miss Clement, do let me know if at any time you've any troubles, or need my help in anything?"

"But of course," she murmured gratefully, knowing he really meant it. Still—that "Miss Clement!" After eight months it might by now have become "Lily". Seeing he was already starting work she went back to her room.

Mr Pelham's day followed its usual course, till at a quarter to six he squared up his papers, pressed his desk-bell and rose from his chair.

"I'm off now, Miss Clement," he said, as she came in. "There are a few things still on my desk, but you can deal with them tomorrow, if you want to get along."

He was just on his way out when he heard a reproachful little "Oh!" Lily Clement had found the Manson folder exactly where he had put it that morning and with no draft letter or other indication that anything had been done, clipped on the outside.

"What is it?" he asked a little shamefacedly, well knowing. "Oh that. I've gone through it… Well, I've been thinking it over and I can't quite see the correct decision yet."

"But surely their proposal——"

"Oh, it looks all right on the surface. But it's not exactly, well, conservative, is it?"

"One never gets anywhere by being too fearfully conservative."

"Not even into trouble," he laughed. "Anyway, I promise you I'll sleep on it. Night-night!"

A few moments later, he was standing in Bedford Street with uplifted umbrella. A taxi was soon in front of him.

"Savernake Club," he told the driver after a moment's hesitation. It had been in his mind to see a new film at the Gaumont Cinema which had had good notices—he was a fairly regular film-goer—but remembered it would make him too late to go home for dinner, and

Rogerson would be put out if it were called off at this hour. He was an excellent cook and took great pleasure in well-planned and well-served meals. Moreover, Pelham invariably let him know by lunchtime if he was going to be out. He decided on a game of billiards at the Club instead.

In the entrance hall, Gough, the hall-porter, handed him a letter. It was for an overdue bill at which he was slightly annoyed. Not at the bill itself but because he had somehow missed paying it, and it was his habit to deal promptly with all matters involving finance. He made a little note about the bill in his diary under tomorrow's date and wandered downstairs to the billiard-room.

Both tables were occupied and his friend Paddy, the marker, who was scoring at one of them, gave him a quick, humorously commiserating little signal, indicating that the games had only just started. He sat down and waited. After five minutes a Colonel Bellamy with whom he often played came in and took a seat beside him.

"Hullo, Jim! Going to let me have my revenge for last Friday as soon as a table's vacant?"

Pelham reflected. The players were not very good, would take some time, and Bellamy who considered himself, with not much justification, an accomplished raconteur was apt to start anecdotes and hold up the game while he told them.

"Don't think so, old man. If a table had been free—but I have to be home by seven-thirty."

"As you like. By the way, chap told me a good one at lunch. It seems there was a Scotsman came to London for the first time…"

Pelham listened politely, laughed heartily at the end—for it was quite funny, though he wished he could have heard the original story, not his friend's obviously lengthier version—and then wandered upstairs to the bar on the first floor.

Here, over a dry sherry, he fell into conversation with two other acquaintances on various subjects dear to businessmen's hearts—the iniquity of the Government, of trade union restrictive practices, and of taxation—passing thence to the general state of trade and finally to the latest smart deal the speaker had pulled off. Pelham joined in unobtrusively here and there, quite enjoying himself and thinking what nice chaps they were, accepted another sherry but stood out of ensuing rounds, and when it came to the question of deals felt obliged, suddenly recalling the Manson folder in his tray, to strike a cautious note to the assembly at large.

"I don't know, old boy. I see your point, but one's got to go carefully these days."

"Go too carefully, Pell, and you'll never get anywhere."

Miss Clement, Pelham thought, would have approved of the speaker. "I mean, take reasonable business risks, but don't make hasty decisions."

"Hey! What about Disraeli and the Suez Canal shares? He bought 'em for the country by telegram. One of the best deals ever made—at least up to 1956—and if that wasn't a hasty decision…"

"All very well in those days," retorted Pelham with spirit, "but with the state of the world now things are different. You've only got to make a couple of false moves and you're out in the street."

"Pell, the Apostle of Caution!" They all laughed, but there was no malice. Though they might think him unenterprising, he was much too kindly a little man for anyone really to dislike.

After a short while longer, Pelham glanced at his watch and left. Although he hadn't had his game of billiards, he had enjoyed his talk and his two glasses of sherry and felt at peace with all the world. He even hummed cheerfully to himself as he went down the stairs.

It was seven o'clock on Wednesday, 8th May. He did not know that he was just about to receive the first intimation of the great change that was going to come over his whole simple, happy, humdrum life, the tiny almost unnoticed wind-ripple that so lightly brushes a field of wheat but is nevertheless the unrecognised herald of a devastating storm.

3

I n the hall, Pelham got his hat and umbrella and was about to tell Gough to send a page for a taxi when he saw one drawing up at the kerb and hurried outside.

"Why, hullo, Camberly!" He had recognised the descending passenger.

"Hello there, Pell! Buying my cab off me?"

"Yes. I've got to get along, or I'd love a chat. Haven't seen you for ages."

The other chuckled. "*That's* true enough. But I've seen *you*."

"Me? When was this?"

"Oh, one day last week. Leicester Square way—about seven-thirty." He gave the driver a pound note and stood waiting impatiently while the man initiated a leisurely and slightly resentful pocket-by-pocket search for change. "You were coming out of the pictures."

"But—let me see! I didn't go to a film at all last week."

"Oh! I thought you were with a bunch of people just leaving. You had that bewildered look—you know, one minute you're watching the final clinch and wishing it was you, and next you're out in the cold hard street. But you may only have been passing."

"Ah. That'll be it I should think." On leaving the office Pelham sometimes, if it was a fine evening, walked a short part of the way home, going to the top end of Bedford Street and turning left into New Row. This tiny thoroughfare with a roadway only seven-foot-wide always delighted him because in its short length it had nearly every possible type of shop from baker, hairdresser, grocer and milliner down to laundry, dairy, snack bar and even a theatrical costumier's. By it he came out into St Martin's Lane and so across it to Leicester Square, somewhere between which point and Piccadilly Circus he began to look for a taxi. And he had certainly done this last week, but

16

which day he couldn't remember. "Sorry I didn't see you," he added. "I must have been dreaming."

"That's O.K. I only had time to wave vaguely at you across the crowd. I was in a tearing hurry. I am now, too, by George." He received his change, gave a tip, and started up the steps.

"Here! Wait!" called Pelham. "Did you say seven-thirty?"

"Round about. And it was Wednesday—I remember now, because I was dashing off to the theatre."

"I wouldn't have been passing there as late as that on any day. Besides," he recollected with sudden triumph, "on that particular evening I was at a sherry-party in Hampstead. Couldn't have been me."

"Oh well! I'll forgive you then. So long! Must rush." He disappeared inside the Club.

Smiling to himself Pelham registered a mental note to make some little quip, when next they met, about Camberly needing to get his eyesight tested, climbed into the waiting taxi, and gave the address of his flat.

"Good evening, sir." Rogerson, as was his invariable custom on hearing his master's key in the door, had appeared in the hall from the passage to the left which led to the kitchen. He relieved Pelham of his hat and umbrella and went on: "A Mrs Van Heston phoned shortly after six."

"Van Heston?"

"An American lady I judge, sir, from her speech."

"Oh, of course." Mrs Van Heston was representing a New York firm with whom Pelham Lake and Co had dealings. He had heard she was coming over in the early summer but hadn't expected her so soon.

"I understood her to say she had just—er—flown in today. She phoned your office but you had already gone, so Miss Clement gave her your number here."

"Ah yes, quite right. I have to meet her while she's over."

"She left a message, sir, saying she had only ten days in London and was filling up her book, so could you fix your date with her as soon as possible. She added that perhaps you would phone her this evening. She also added"—Rogerson had, by now, a faraway look in his face, as of one trying to recall the essential points of a somewhat complicated

17

conversation— "that Tuesday next would suit her best, further adding that she could make it Monday if Tuesday didn't suit; or if Monday was impossible, perhaps this coming Friday."

Pelham, already amused, now laughed out loud as Rogerson with a faint twitch of the lips played what was obviously his trump card. "She then rang off before I could inquire her telephone number."

"But how on earth…"

"It's all right, sir," Rogerson reassured him. "Fortunately she realised the situation she had created and phoned back a few minutes later to add that she was staying at the Savoy and could be reached there any time this evening."

Pelham recalled the precise and straightforward business correspondence he had invariably had with Mrs Van Heston, and came to the conclusion that she must possess a pretty efficient secretary. He looked at his diary where the only Tuesday entry was "Rogerson—five years today", and said, "Yes, Tuesday's all right. I think I'll take her to lunch somewhere smart. American women like being taken to smart places, don't they?"

"I do not know particularly about American women, sir, but I'd say it was true of all women," replied Rogerson with a grave twinkle. "As the more ornamental sex they appreciate a bright setting."

Pelham was secretly intrigued at his staid manservant unexpectedly talking in a worldly way about women. He tried to visualise Rogerson with a girl and simply could not. Even when younger—if he'd ever been any younger. He still looked exactly the same as when he entered Pelham's service five years ago and gave the impression of having been the same for years before that.

"I'll phone her right away then," he said and went into the room on the left.

"Shall I get you a glass of sherry, sir?" asked Rogerson, following to the door.

"No, thanks. I've had two at the Club." Pelham was by nature abstemious, though what he drank was always good, and he preferred wine to spirits, which he rarely touched, though he kept whisky handy in the flat for visitors. He sat down by the phone and was soon listening to Mrs Van Heston's warm enthusiastic voice flowing relentlessly over

18

his half-finished sentences like summer rain down a window. Barely indeed was he able to insinuate his lunch invitation for Tuesday, the sole object of his ringing up, so pleased did she seem to be at actually talking to him in person—for they had never met—after all the letters they had exchanged in the last months.

She rang off at last, leaving him to wonder a little ruefully what the lunch was going to be like, if this were a sample of her conversational powers, yet already drawn to the friendly personality which had projected itself over the wire.

Five minutes later, when he had just left his bedroom after changing into a soft collar and a lighter tie than his dark business one, as was his usual evening custom, the phone rang again. It was Mrs Van Heston once more. Evidently it was her custom to make two phone calls do the work of one, for she said as if there had been no interruption whatever: "Oh, and by the way, Mr Pelham, as we've never had the pleasure of meeting, how shall I know you on Tuesday?"

"Well," he replied, at a loss how to describe himself, "I'm not very tall, and I have a little moustache, and... But I'll wear a white flower in my buttonhole to make it easier." All the same, he thought, as he put the receiver down and sat there half expecting it to ring yet again, he'd probably recognise her before she did him. A woman like she seemed to be must stand out a mile, while he—he smiled self-deprecatingly—was the sort of chap who needed a button-hole before anyone even noticed he was there.

He was quite right. When he entered the cocktail bar of the restaurant he had selected, he observed plenty of women but only one who could be Mrs Van Heston. She was middle-aged, large and comfortable, yet perfectly dressed, with a twinkling friendly eye, and as Pelham came up to the table where she was sitting she embarked on a sentence of welcome which lasted so long that the waiter, hovering to take their order, at last gave up in despair and began to dwindle into the background.

"Mr Pelham! At last! If this isn't just the loveliest kind of meeting! I mean after knowing each other on paper and from a strictly business angle, to meet in such pleasant surroundings, and really get to know each other face to face... No. I know what you're going to say. That I don't look like what you expected... That's very kind of you but it's not true... Now how did I visualize you, you're next going to ask..." It was only the sight of the departing waiter that enabled Pelham to stem the flood by calling after him and asking her what she would drink.

His carefully chosen lunch was, he was delighted to observed, much appreciated by his guest. Evidently, she understood good food and also seemed knowledgeable about wine. He had been rather afraid that she might, like some Americans he knew, smoke between each course and drown everything with gallons of iced water.

Over the meal they discussed business, and by the time they were relaxing over coffee and Grand Marnier, Pelham's regard for his companion was tinged with respect. Exuding good fellowship and verbosity like an overfull bath sponge, Mrs Van Heston yet had all her wits about her and he realised he had given way on one or two points which he had not intended to concede. Never mind, he'd thoroughly enjoyed the meeting and considered she was quite charming. In fact, he was having a very pleasant day; and there was still the evening to come, to which he was quite looking forward.

For the presentation of the cigarette-case that morning had gone off most satisfactorily. Rogerson had been obviously taken by surprise, had appeared quite touched by the gift, and had dutifully smiled at the "little quip" on the card. "I shall most certainly treasure this, sir," he had said, "not so much for itself as for the thought behind it. May I take it you will be dining at home tonight, or should I wait till lunch-time to know for certain?"

The juxtaposition of ideas had told Pelham something was in the wind. He at once guessed that Rogerson had conceived the idea of a rather special dinner for that evening, as his own way of marking the occasion.

"Yes, I'll definitely stay at home tonight, Rogerson. After lunch with my American lady I shan't be sorry to have a quiet evening, I expect."

That had been certainly true. Delightful though the lunch had been, it had also been exhausting, as he only now had leisure to realise, Mrs Van Heston having been unaccountably silent for nearly two minutes, slowly sipping her liqueur. In another moment, however, she came briskly into action again, gathering up her bag.

"Well, now I really must fly off, Mr Pelham. I have a whole raft of appointments to keep in London before I move over to Paris at the end of the week. I just can't begin to tell you how much I've enjoyed our little meeting…" All the same she promptly began, and continued to do so the whole time they were getting up and making their way between the tables to the door, till Pelham had to interrupt with a "Hullo!" to a man at a table they were passing who had half-risen and greeted him.

He made the introductions. "Mr MacAndrew—a business friend of mine," he explained to his guest.

"I was wondering if we still were friends, Jim," laughed the other. "You see," he continued to Mrs Van Heston, "a few days ago he gave me the dirtiest cut I've ever had. Walked right past me."

"I did?" Pelham was staggered. "Oh, nonsense!"

"True as you're here now. Only last Friday. No, wait! I think it was Thursday."

"I'm extremely sorry. I suppose I just didn't see you."

"You saw me all right. Why, we were looking at each other all the time we approached. And when I said, 'Hullo Jim!' you merely stared in my face and then walked on."

"I haven't known Mr Pelham long," put in Mrs Van Heston, "but that seems to me about the last thing he'd ever do. A real kindly nature is the way I'd…"

Thoroughly upset, Pelham unceremoniously interrupted her. "It can't have been me," he stated indignantly.

MacAndrew, nothing if not outspoken, retorted: "I'd know that dial of yours anywhere, old man. I've seen quite a bit of it in my time."

"Well, well," said Mrs Van Heston, quite intrigued. "What do you know?"

"Besides, it was at the bottom end of Bedford Street, just a hundred yards from your office, at a quarter to one."

Yes, just about the time he'd be going out to lunch, thought Pelham. But how could he possibly have been greeted by MacAndrew, looked straight at him, and walked on? Unless he was completely wrapped up in his own thoughts?

"Something on his mind perhaps, Mr MacAndrew." Mrs Van Heston evidently had the same idea. "Business worries. We all have them. I remember once when our firm had a tricky lawsuit on, I did much the same thing twice in one day."

"Maybe," conceded the other. "Now I come to think of it he did look as if he didn't quite realise where he was. Sort of preoccupied."

But Pelham knew he hadn't had any really worrying problems on hand lately, and anyway he was not the kind of person who let business intrude too much on his thoughts outside the office. "I'm absolutely convinced it can't have been me," he cut in. "But just at that time and place when you might so easily expect to see me, perhaps you..." But MacAndrew was smiling and shaking his head. "Oh, well! Anyway, Mac, I'm frightfully sorry about it, whoever it really was."

"And I won't hold it against you—or whoever it really was," grinned MacAndrew. "We all do it. I just thought I'd pull your leg about it... Mrs Van Heston, I do apologize for intruding, but I wanted to make certain I hadn't been cut out of his visiting list without knowing why."

"That's O.K. I quite understand. But I guess we're keeping you from your meal. Goodbye!" Followed by Pelham, feeling rather worried, she continued out of the restaurant.

"Does that sort of thing often happen in London?" she asked amusedly, as her taxi was being called.

"I should hope not. It's the first time it's ever..." He broke off. "Now that's funny!" He had just remembered his encounter with Camberly a few days before.

"What's funny?"

"A short while ago another fellow thought he'd seen me too. But it turned out he was definitely mistaken. I wasn't within a mile of the place."

"Well, this time you were, and somebody did see you, and *you* didn't see *him*. Don't let it bother you," she added kindly, seeing he was still a little ruffled. "Darn it all, we can't go around all day with our eyes on stalks in case someone we know is passing. You just forget it right now! Well, good-bye, and thank you again for the best meal yet."

But Pelham found himself unable to forget the incident quite so easily as all that and continued to puzzle over it in his taxi. By the time he had reached Bedford Street, however, he had realised that, even if he had by some extraordinary chance failed to greet a friend in the street, it was absurd to worry about it. MacAndrew was the person most concerned, and he hadn't minded in the least, had only, as he said, been pulling his leg. With a little shrug he put it definitely out of his mind, paid off the taxi, and slowly climbed the stairs to his office, wishing now that he hadn't had quite such a good lunch.

4

Pelham treated himself to a newsreel for an hour after leaving the office and then went straight home. He must be in good time for the special little dinner that he knew was being got ready for him.

He let himself into his flat to a faint smell of most enticing cooking, which explained why Rogerson for once did not make his usual appearance in the hall at the sound of his master's return. On this particular evening he obviously had more important matters on hand in the kitchen.

Pelham went to his bedroom to change his collar and tie. There he had a sudden inspiration, and instead put on a dinner-jacket in honour of the occasion. Taking a glass of sherry later in the sitting-room he was rewarded by the expression of surprise instantly followed by gratification which came over Rogerson's face when he entered to announce that dinner would be ready in ten minutes.

"Meanwhile, sir, I came to ask what wine you would wish to drink."

Evidently in Rogerson's opinion the occasion merited wine, so Pelham went one better. "Champagne, I think, is called for, Rogerson. Have we any of the Mumm left?"

"Only the Pol Roger now, sir."

"Then let it be that. And afterwards I'd like you to take a glass with me and we'll drink each other's health."

"You are very kind, sir." He hesitated a moment at the door. "And may I thank you once again for the handsome gift. I was a little too overwhelmed this morning to express myself adequately."

"That's all right," Pelham said kindly, thinking how easy it was to make other people happy by being a little thoughtful, and how happy it made one oneself.

"I went out at once to purchase some cigarettes to fill it, as I had almost run out."

"Good!" smiled Pelham. It occurred to him that some manservants might have taken Pelham's cigarettes for the purpose, but Rogerson was as honest as daylight. So far from having occasionally to check the whisky and sherry decanters, which regretfully he'd had to do with his predecessor, Pelham had put the entire cellar in his charge.

"But, as I said this morning, sir, not the gift but the thought," went on Rogerson, quite abruptly for him, and left the room.

Ten minutes later he reappeared, opening the connecting door to the little dining-room and announced dinner. He always did this: he was as much a stickler for formality and the proper way of running a gentleman's household, whether a flat or a Stately Home of England, as Pelham himself.

Pelham went in. Rogerson had really surpassed himself. Silver winked against the polished table, a large silver bowl had been brought out of retirement, cleaned till it shone like the moon and filled with flowers, glasses gleamed, and there was a napkinned champagne bottle in ice on the sideboard. And facing Pelham's chair was a little white card headed "Anniversary Menu" in Rogerson's neat hand. There were no fewer than five courses.

Pelham sat down feeling like a benevolent little king receiving homage and distributing largesse.

But halfway through the meal his mind unexpectedly and annoyingly reverted to his encounter with MacAndrew. What had really worried him, he now recognised, was not the actual ignoring of his friend; it was that he was convinced he could never have been so preoccupied as to have walked blindly past anybody after being actually greeted face to face. And now he had remembered something. Thursday, he thought, was the day Mac had said he'd seen him going to lunch. But on Thursday, surely, he'd been down at Chislehurst on business, leaving at ten and not getting back till four. He felt that for his own peace of mind he must clear the point up immediately.

Rogerson, entering proudly at that moment with a sweet omelette, was rather put out to be told to leave it and go at once and fetch his master's diary from the dressing-table. And when he had done so and had set the dish on the table, Pelham paid no attention to it till he had consulted an entry. Yes, Thursday had been his Chislehurst day. Then he couldn't have been seen by MacAndrew in Bedford Street at a quarter to one.

Roused by a hurt cough from Rogerson he started on the omelette in a much brighter frame of mind, till a new thought came to worry him. Was it after all Thursday that MacAndrew had said? Or was it Friday? He had mentioned one day first and then corrected himself to the other, but Pelham couldn't remember now in what order. And if it wasn't Thursday the matter was still just where it had been. He must ring MacAndrew and verify the point as soon as possible. To Rogerson's perturbation he hurried through the rest of the meal and only just, as he was going out of the room, recollected his promise to drink mutual healths.

"If you don't mind waiting a moment, Rogerson," he apologized. "But I've remembered an important bit of business. I must phone at once or the fellow will be gone."

That was a lie, he realised, as he hurried from the room: it was really that he couldn't wait. And anyway once he'd confirmed that it had been Thursday and not Friday, he'd be in a better frame of mind for health-drinking and a friendly chat with Rogerson.

He got MacAndrew at last. He and his wife were dining out with friends but Pelham had got the number from a sitter-in. Already he was feeling a little ashamed at thus chasing him up on such a small matter.

"Mac? It's me—Jim Pelham! Terribly sorry to ring you like this, when you're somebody's guest and…"

"Not at all, old man, not at all." MacAndrew had been dining well obviously: that was a help. "Something important?"

"Well, no, not really. It's merely about that day when you said I didn't see you."

"Oh, that! That's O.K., Jim old boy! Who cares? Good Lord! If people can't…"

"No, it's not quite that. Did you say it was Thursday or Friday?"

"Thursday, Friday, Saturday, Sunday, what's it matter? You aren't really worrying about… But it was definitely Thursday now I come to think of it."

"You're certain?" Pelham couldn't keep the relief out of his voice.

"Dead certain. Tell you why. I nearly always lunch Fleet Street way, but on Thursday I'd fixed to meet a chap at the Charing Cross Hotel and was on my way there when I saw you."

"Aha!" Pelham was triumphant. "Then it couldn't have been me. I was at Chislehurst all day."

"Nonsense! It was *you* I… Oh!" He laughed at himself. "I see your point. If you weren't there it couldn't have been. Still, it was the most extraordinary resemblance. You must have a double is all I can, say. Good God! Two Jim Pelhams in one world! Appalling thought!"

He laughed again and Pelham laughed too. "I'm glad to have got it straight, Mac. I knew I couldn't have cut you… Well, so long! Sorry to have been such a nuisance."

Much happier, he returned to the dining-room, where Rogerson was waiting. He poured out two glasses of champagne in which they formally toasted each other and Pelham congratulated him on the dinner. "It makes me wish we had an anniversary every week," he said; and then, with the phone conversation fresh in his mind, added: "I say, Rogerson, do you think I'm the sort of chap to have a double?"

"A double, sir?" Rogerson was all at sea. "A double what?"

Pelham laughed. "I don't mean a double whisky or anything. Someone exactly like me, who could be mistaken for me?"

Rogerson considered his master reflectively—the small rather precise figure, neatly brushed dark hair, little moustache and round kindly face. Must be hundreds like him, he thought. Aloud he said, emboldened by champagne: "Well, sir, if you'll excuse me saying it, you *are* rather the type. Your hair is arranged and moustache trimmed in a manner common to many other business gentlemen, which immediately provides a superficial likeness. And your…"

"I mean *very* like, not superficially. Could someone meet me face to face and speak to me, when"—he found he'd started his sentence wrongly—"when it wasn't me at all, if you see what I mean?"

Rogerson considered again. "Well frankly, sir, yes, I think he might. Though naturally he'd soon realise his mistake."

"Ah yes, of course! Have some more champagne?" He felt a little guilty now at having rather spoilt Rogerson's meal by his preoccupation with that MacAndrew incident. It was just his over-sensitiveness, his desire to be on perpetual friendly terms with everyone and his annoyance at being put in the false position, through no fault of his own, of having for some days been thought capable of cutting his friends. Really, they ought to have known instinctively he wasn't that sort.

But when Rogerson had finished his second glass and Pelham had returned to the sitting-room, he once more began to feel worried. A new aspect of the affair had crossed his mind. Supposing there *was* someone in London, as there seemed to be, so like him as to be mistaken for him, he might be held responsible for what that person did. Indeed, he had been twice already, though it had been satisfactorily cleared up and wasn't in any case very much. But suppose this man was at this moment reeling drunk down Piccadilly, perhaps to be seen by one of Pelham's club acquaintances? He, Pelham, would get the blame and, unlike the two simple incidents which had already occurred, might not hear anything about it. It was one thing for a friend to say, "Why did you cut me on Thursday?" It would have to be a very real friend—or else an enemy, though he didn't think he possessed any—who would say, "You were making a pretty exhibition of yourself in Piccadilly last night, Jim, weren't you?"

No, all sorts of things might happen and he would never learn about them. It was rather a terrifying thought and he went to bed in a somewhat subdued frame of mind.

Next morning, however, he woke to the realization that he had let his imagination run away with him a bit. Too much champagne at dinner, he told himself severely, on the top of sherry, burgundy, and liqueurs at lunch, had by the end of the day undoubtedly affected his sense of proportion. Just because some harmless and quite unwitting stranger had on a couple of occasions been mistaken for him, and the laughing remark had been made that he must have a double, he'd built up a sort of Jekyll-and-Hyde drama in which a debauched roué staggered evilly round London getting the staid and innocent Pelham blamed for his misdeeds. He felt quite ashamed of himself. There must be dozens of people in London who closely resembled someone else without anything at all ever coming of it beyond perhaps an occasional amusing little misunderstanding. Indeed, it was rather something to joke about than to worry over in the absurd way he had the previous evening. Tentatively he toyed with the idea of looking MacAndrew straight in the eye when next he met him and saying: "Excuse me, I'm not J. M. Pelham: I'm his double." And he could make some little quip to Miss Clement, after he'd told her about it of course, to the effect that she'd better be careful how she spoke to him if she happened to see him in the street, because it mightn't be him at all.

But this he never did, for when he arrived at the office that Wednesday morning, there was a phone message from the girl Lily Clement shared rooms with to say she couldn't come to work as she'd got flu. She'd be back as soon as she could and hoped Mr Pelham would be able to carry on without her.

The result of this was that in a couple of days the whole question of the possible existence of a double had been driven right out of Pelham's head, for he found small time to think of anything but the work in the office. He hadn't realised how much he had come to depend on his secretary's quiet efficiency. There was so much she had at her fingertips which the rest of his staff didn't know; and the substitute, whom he'd immediately got in for dictation and typing, was a dashing blonde who continually made eyes at him—or at least Pelham thought she did. This reduced him to a state of embarrassed shyness in which he couldn't marshal his thoughts properly. Miss Clement, he found himself reflecting on more than one occasion, never crossed her legs when sitting quite so revealingly as that.

That evening Pelham in his kindly fashion went all the way to Fulham where Lily Clement lived in order to take her some flowers and a note begging her not to come back a moment before she was really quite fit again.

Joyce, her companion, who took them in at the door, was terrifically impressed by the gesture—in more ways than Pelham knew. Indeed, it was just as well he didn't hear the subsequent conversation through the open door of Lily's bedroom, Joyce keeping at a distance for fear of infection.

"If my boss did a thing like that, I'd know what to think."

29

"What?" came the rather shivery response. Lily was feeling very sorry for herself but had been immensely cheered by the flowers and the heart-warming little note.

"That he was sweet on me. I mean, in his position and all that way down here."

"Then you'd be wrong. You don't know Mr Pelham like I do. It's just his kindness."

"You be careful, Lil! Or he'll…"

"Don't be silly!"

"Mind you, he isn't married. That's something in his favour."

"Why is it in his favour?" The flu had made Lily a little slow in the uptake.

"Because if he was married, it'd only mean one thing. Not being, it can mean two. Though I doubt it," she added, frankly. "Still, he's not too old, you know."

"Oh, you're talking nonsense, Joyce. Besides, you're forgetting Jack."

Joyce burst out laughing. "Oh, darling, I'm only teasing you. Of course I'm not forgetting Boy Friend. But you aren't engaged—even though you have been going out with him for so long."

"I know," replied Lily faintly.

"But you're in love with Jack all right, aren't you?"

"Oh, *yes*."

"And he's in love with you, if I know anything about it—and I certainly do. Why *don't* you get properly fixed up?"

Lily gave a wan little smile. "He hasn't asked me yet. And it is up to him."

"Then why doesn't he get up to it?"

"I think it's money. He's not earning very much at present… Well, it'd be enough really as far as I'm concerned, but he wants to do things well always, not just scrape along."

"I see. Still, I don't think it's fair on you, keeping you hanging on."

"Oh, I don't know." A little exhausted by the conversation, Lily closed her eyes and relapsed into thought. In her heart she knew well that Jack, who was only twenty-five, would ask her to marry him in his own good time. It was absurd to say that he was being unfair to her. She loved him; and, more, she was eternally grateful to him. For actually, when Lily was about twenty-one and first came to London, on her widower father's death, from a rigorously strait-laced upbringing in a Midland town, she had promptly fallen passionately for a man whom she had believed equally in love with her. For a fortnight they went everywhere together, whenever it was possible, and then she discovered that he had a wife. Even so, such was her infatuation, the unsuspected urgings of a hitherto strictly inhibited desirousness, that she had begged him to get divorced and marry her, or to run away with her, or to make her his mistress, anything to satisfy her hunger for him. The man, who had only looked on her as a pleasant companion to kiss and cuddle on the side, mere nourishment for his male vanity, thereupon abruptly threw her over, frightened not only of her scenes and wild pleadings but of her avid and uncontrolled passion. Technically, she had kept her virtue, or rather he had done so for her, but for nearly a year she had lived with the bitter shameful memory of the whole episode, afraid of herself and that sudden brief upsurge of latent madness in her blood.

Then Jack Benton had come along and with a steady persistent friendship, gradually turning into devotion, had restored her to normal life, helped her, unknowingly, to conquer herself. The horrible, humiliating business had vanished from her mind as though it had never been. He had given her back her assurance, her confidence in her own powers of self-control. She knew that with him she would be as happy and safe as any woman could be—protected by a home, adoring husband, children—really at peace.

She snuggled luxuriously in her bed; in spite of the flu she felt so contented with life, so much in love. Opening her eyes, she realised that Joyce had thought she'd dropped off to sleep and had quietly shut the door leaving her alone. In a few more minutes she did drop off.

5

Lily Clement did not come back to work till the following Wednesday. She would have come on Monday but Pelham had practically ordered her not to. "Flu needs a full week to get over it, and I'm going on perfectly well by myself," he had written her—a considerable distortion of the truth this last, for he was in a great muddle. But he had had flu two or three times himself and hated every minute of it and so felt extremely sympathetic to any other sufferer. Besides," he had added, "with this beastly weather"—it had rained solidly for five days—"you're better off at home, even if you were in perfect health."

Wednesday, however, was suddenly a perfect day, so much so that Pelham couldn't bear the thought of the tube and instead took a taxi, telling the driver to drive eastwards past Lord's and slowly down through the west side of Regent's Park. It was a blaze of tulips and flowering shrubs, backed by the new young green of the trees bordering the ornamental water, and he felt that life could hardly be more pleasant.

"Well! Well! Welcome back to Pelham Lake and Co!" he cried, as he entered the office to see his secretary placing some papers on his desk. He was so pleased that she was really back and that he was at last free of the oncoming blonde that he found himself unaccountably shaking hands. "Are you sure you're quite well again?"

"Perfectly, thanks! And it doesn't seem to have been the kind of flu that leaves you limp for days afterwards. I'm ready for anything."

"You mustn't leave me alone again… What are these flowers on the desk? Did you put them there?"

"They're a little present for you," she admitted shyly. "After your kindness in giving *me* flowers and coming all that way twice to bring them." For Pelham had repeated his visit on the Saturday—much to Joyce's amusement.

32

"But Miss Clement!" Pelham was deeply touched and patted her shoulder affectionately. "You really shouldn't."

Lily was quite startled at the touch. Almost paternal though the gesture was, it had never happened before. She wished Joyce could have been there to see it. She would have understood Mr Pelham better. Or would she? She'd more likely have said: "You watch that fatherly stuff, Lil! It's the way they all begin." For after that second gift of flowers Joyce had stated that she was convinced that Mr Pelham's motives were dishonourable; and Lily didn't know whether she was teasing or really believed it. Joyce's experience with her various employers—assuming she had reported them accurately—had been startling, to say the least of it; and Lily just couldn't make her understand that Mr Pelham was, if anything, far too much the other way—terribly kind, but otherwise so shy and impersonal in his relations with her that it made her feel like a well-tended machine. Only the previous evening she had informed Joyce quite tartly, when Mr Pelham and his intentions had again cropped up: "But I tell you, he's the simple type." To which that young lady had replied darkly: "Those simple ones are sometimes the deepest. Wait till he starts making passes!"

Passes! Mr Pelham! Looking at him as he turned away to smell the flowers, she nearly laughed out loud. Such an idea, she knew, could never enter his head.

"Now we really must get to work," she announced briskly. "I expect there's any amount of things you want to put me wise about."

But Pelham wasn't in the mood for work just yet. "In a moment," he said. "It's far too perfect a day." He looked wistfully at the sunlight on the carpet to the left of his desk. "Just think how lovely it'd be at Kew." An idea struck him. "You know I'm a brutal employer—keeping you in on such a wonderful morning. Especially when you've just got up after flu. You ought to be out in the sun, convalescing. Wouldn't you like to go off? I can muddle along for just another day."

"Of course I couldn't. The idea!"

"Think of it, though! Kew! In May!" The glorious morning seemed to have made Pelham slightly mad. "Perhaps you could get your boy-friend to..." He broke off. "I hope I haven't put my foot in it. You *have* got a boyfriend, haven't you? I seem to remember your mentioning it once."

"Oh yes, I've got one," she replied happily.

"Excellent! Is he a nice respectable young man?"

"His name's Jack Benton and he's a confidential clerk with Hayes and Holbrook. In Fleet Street, you know."

He nodded. "He sounds *most* respectable. And what's he like to look at?"

"Dark and not very tall. For a man, that is—he's the same height as me. He wears glasses and has a very clever face. Well, he *is* clever, come to that."

"But of course. Funny, though, I thought he was big and fair-haired: at least I met a young chap once outside the office who said he was waiting for you and I wondered if…"

"Oh, that'd be my brother, Tom. He's quite different. Not so clever, but very strong and—you know, tough." Delighted by his sudden interest in her affairs she expanded further. "He nearly stayed on in the Army after his National Service in order to be a Commando, but without a full-scale war he said there was no future in it."

"A most useful protector for a lone young lady."

"I don't know about that. He's inclined to protect me too much. I mean he sort of puts me on a pedestal. One day when we were out together…" She broke off, realising she was talking an awful lot. It was probably the effect of getting back to her kindly Mr Pelham and the office after a week's absence. Most certainly she was enjoying it: it was undoubtedly establishing the sort of companionship she felt ought to exist between them. But he might not be seeing it that way. "I—I must be boring you with all this?" she ventured.

"Not at all. Go on!"

"Well, a man started staring at me—nothing more than the usual thing that often happens to girls in public, you know…"

"Only to the pretty ones," interjected Pelham, still apparently under the influence of the morning.

Considerably startled at this unprecedented gallantry from her usually staid employer, Lily smiled a gratified acknowledgement. "Yes, in its way it *is* a kind of compliment, and one takes it in one's stride.

But just because it was his sister, Tom wanted to go over and hit him." Her face clouded. "He's *too* tough, if you see what I mean. He believes in force as an argument. Too many American gangster films, I expect. You know: 'Lookit, bud! You keep outa our territory, or else…'"

The sudden harsh words in a fake American accent coming from his pretty and demure secretary's lips made Mr Pelham laugh.

"I'm serious, really. It's his great fault, but he knows it now, thank Heaven. That's why he's taken the job he has. Something in which he just has to be polite to people."

"And what is that?"

"I know it sounds funny after what I've just said, but he's a car salesman."

"Lookit, bud! You buy this car, or else…" grinned Pelham, very pleased with his little quip, and more so when Lily laughed delightedly.

"He works in outer London, but he comes to see me and take me out occasionally."

"I see. And your Jack Benton. You're engaged to him, I take it?"

"Well, actually, not yet," replied Lily, smiling radiantly.

"Ah! An understanding! Well, I hope the wedding won't be too soon. From a purely selfish point of view, of course. I shan't find another secretary like you in a hurry."

Lily flushed with pleasure. "I too hope I won't have to desert you yet awhile. I'm too interested in the work. And talking of work, you're egging me on to gossip when there's such heaps to do."

Pelham sighed. He'd enjoyed the little conversation, so in keeping with the bright May morning. "You're a hard taskmaster, Miss Clement."

Miss Clement! Lily pouted to herself. Even after he'd encouraged her to confide in him about Jack and her brother in such an informal way. "There's the morning's mail, Mr Pelham," she said, pointedly formal. "One letter is marked 'Personal' which I haven't opened. I've got a lot of other stuff outside—things that cropped up while I was away; I'd like to run through them quickly before I bring them in. And I've a note to remind you about the Manson business, but I can't find the folder."

Pelham opened a drawer. "It's here," he said, a little defiantly.

Lily was upset. "Do you mean you've decided nothing yet? You are awful," she added before she could stop herself. But then she was feeling rather differently towards him after that friendly little talk. "I mean, it's been in the office over a fortnight now."

"Oh, I rang them and said I needed a good deal of time to consider it. But, you know, I don't like it somehow." He looked at her thoughtfully. "You're a smart girl. What would *you* do about it?"

"Accept their proposition. But"—she took the folder, studied it for a moment, then laid a finger against a paragraph—"get them to agree to wash out that clause."

"But that's a safeguard for *us*."

"Not if the *whole* thing comes off—instead of only the Gutteridge side of it—as it may well do. It'll be a handicap then and you won't do nearly so well out of it."

"It frightens me rather."

"You mustn't *be* frightened." Carried away, she was speaking very earnestly. "Please, Mr Pelham, you must be more—more ambitious. I do so want the firm to get really ahead, expand, become more and more important. If one always tries to keep in the same place, one slowly slips back. But of course it's for you to decide," she ended lightly, a little ashamed of her outburst, and hurriedly left the room.

Pelham found himself quite touched by his secretary's unexpected display of loyal enthusiasm. He hadn't realised she cared so much about the firm she had only been with for eight months. He sat for some minutes staring at the document. "I still don't like it," he said at last, petulantly, and started on his mail.

It was about an hour later that he came upon the letter marked 'Personal'. Opening it, he glanced at the signature and saw it was Ed Travers, a business acquaintance of his with offices in Kingsway. Rather a solid, matter-of-fact type, but Pelham got along very well with him, as indeed he did with most people. Sometimes they lunched together, occasionally met over an evening glass of sherry at a little wine bar called Broad's in St. Martin's Lane, which Travers frequented regularly and Pelham sometimes patronized on the occasional evenings when he walked northwards from the office to pick up a taxi near Leicester Square.

He read the letter, frowned in a puzzled manner and then read it slowly again.

Dear Jim [it ran],
About next Saturday's golf. I know we settled 2.15 at the golf club, but do you think we might leave our respective offices a little early and meet there for lunch? More time for a talk and it'll give us a longer day. Give me a ring which you'd prefer…

Pelham scratched his head helplessly. As he hadn't seen Travers for nearly a fortnight the appointment must have been made by telephone, but he just couldn't recall ever doing so. Maybe with the hectic time he'd been having during Miss Clement's absence it had slipped his memory. He referred to his diary but there was no note about golf on Saturday, such as he would have been sure to have made at the time.

He picked up the phone and called Travers.

"I got your letter about golf, Ed," he began, "but do you know I haven't the faintest recollection of making the arrangement?"

"What?" Travers was surprised.

"My secretary's been down with flu and I've been very rushed. It must have gone right out of my head the moment I put down the phone."

"Phone? What are you talking about? We were in Broad's wine bar. Drinking sherry together. Monday evening. Only the day before yesterday."

This quite staggered Pelham. "But that's impossible. I haven't been there for ten days or more…"

"What on earth do you mean, haven't been there? You were."

"But…" He just didn't know what to make of this. "Well, I seem unaccountably to have forgotten all about it."

"Forgotten? You *can't* have." An idea seemed to strike him. "Unless perhaps you've been overworking—with your girl away and so on, you know?"

"Heavens! I'm not the sort of chap to overwork, would you say?" He essayed a laugh, but it rang hollow: the suggestion that he might have had a complete mental lapse, which seemed at the moment to be the only explanation, quite worried him. "But it *is* rather extraordinary. I'd like to do a bit of checking up. Exactly what time was it we met?"

"Oh, the usual sort of time we do run across one another there. Normally I arrive just after six, and on this occasion I'd just finished my first sherry when you came along. Could be ten minutes later. But I do remember that we left together at a quarter to seven; and you went off towards Leicester Square, as you generally do."

"Thanks. Nothing comes back to me as yet, but…"

"Look here, Jim! Don't let's forget the really important things. About the golf? Do we lunch at the Club or don't we?"

"May I call you back? I'd like to get this thing straight right away."

"Righty-ho, old man. I'm here till one."

Pelham rang off, then promptly rang up his flat. He didn't think it likely Rogerson would be able to help, because he didn't normally discuss his engagements with him, unless they affected the housekeeping, but there was just a chance.

"Rogerson?" he began. "I've got a bit mixed in my recent arrangements. You remember my coming home the day before yesterday, Monday. Soon after seven, I think? Did I say anything to you about a golf appointment next Saturday? I might casually have mentioned it," he added hopefully.

"Monday evening, sir? No, you said nothing to me. But if you'll excuse me, sir, I think you are in error about the time of your return."

"In what way?"

"It was not after seven, sir. You returned more in the neighbourhood of six-fifteen."

"Six-fifteen!" Pelham's voice was sharp.

"I think so, sir. Yes, I'm certain. I recall that I had had trouble with the stove and feared that dinner might be delayed just on the night when you were back earlier than…"

"Oh, all right, all right! Thanks!" cut in Pelham abruptly, and putting the receiver down sat back in his chair.

If he had been home at six-fifteen he couldn't have left a St. Martin's Lane wine bar at six-forty-five. Travers then must have met someone else who… He drew a quick breath. Back into his mind had suddenly come the memory of MacAndrew and Camberly also both meeting someone they had thought was him, someone who, as MacAndrew had suggested, might be his double. Was this same worry going to bob up again when he had completely forgotten about it for a whole week, had considered it over and done with? He stared unhappily at the sunlight on the carpet from which much of the brightness seemed to have gone. He was relieved in a way to know that his memory had not after all been playing him tricks, but the incident was disturbing enough as it was.

Disturbing, he thought further, and puzzling. Because, unlike the other two, Travers had not merely seen the man briefly in the street: he had apparently sat with him for some considerable while, drinking and talking. The voice could hardly have been exactly similar, however much the external appearance was. Yet Travers had been quite definite. And another, even more puzzling, aspect of the matter, now presented itself: why had the stranger talked at all to a man he couldn't have known—even arranged to play golf with him—when he had, and quite naturally, ignored Pelham's other two friends? He must check up on these points right away. He reached once more for the phone.

"About that golf appointment, Ed," he began tentatively. "Something rather funny has happened. It wasn't me you saw the day before yesterday. I was…"

"Not you? It *was*. We had half an hour together, I tell you."

"Sorry. I was at home at the time. I've just checked with my man."

"But, Jim, old boy, we did meet. I can swear to… Who the hell else was it, then?"

"It appears that there's a fellow very like me in circulation in London at the moment. MacAndrew—and you know how well he knows me—mistook him for me ten days ago and so did another chap on another occasion. They thought I'd cut them, to be exact."

"Good Lord! Do you mean I… But no, I can't have done, I'd have sworn…"

"Swear what you like, old man. It wasn't me. But the point is, those two chaps only saw him. You talked to him. Surely his voice wasn't like mine?"

"We-ell, it must have been near enough for me not to suspect." Pelham was surprised at this: it seemed a most extraordinary coincidence. "But, you see," Travers was explaining, "the moment he came in I assumed it *was* you, beckoned him over to have a drink, and never thought any more about it."

"Ah!" Pelham was beginning to form a theory on what had happened. "What did you talk about? Nothing personal to us, I imagine?"

"Personal? Oh, I see! No, it could have been a chat with anyone, looking back on it—the weather, cricket, so on." He chuckled loudly. "What an amazing experience. But I say! The golf! Why on earth did he fix to play golf with a total stranger?"

"That's what I was wondering a moment ago. But I wouldn't mind betting it went like this. You beckoned him over, you say, said 'Hullo, old man!' or something non-committt.al, asked him to have a drink…"

"That's right."

"And he thought, as sometimes people do," continued Pelham triumphantly, for his theory was working out, "that you were an acquaintance he couldn't place for the moment. He stayed talking, hoping to find out. He accepted the golf idea all in good faith, being certain he'd remember who you were before you met again out at the golf club."

"Ye-es. Yes, that does sound reasonable. I've often talked to fellows, racking my brains to think who they were, and after a while it's come to me. Yes, that must be it, because I don't think I ever called him by name, or he'd have realised I was taking him for someone else. And when I suggested our playing golf together, he imagined I was inviting him as a guest. Obviously he can't have been a member of Oxmoor Golf Club or the likeness to you would have been commented on by some of the fellows before now. You know this beats the band." He chuckled again. "And not knowing me really, of course, he'll *never* be able to recall my name. He's in for a bad time. He can't ask for me when he gets to Oxmoor; he'll just have to rely on running into me. I say——" He broke off. "What happens about Saturday now?"

"I'll meet you at two-fifteen." Pelham laughed cheerfully. "I want to meet him too when he turns up."

6

Pelham got to Oxmoor Golf Club earlier than arranged and settled himself in a corner of the veranda where he could see people arriving. He found he was really rather excited. It would be quite an experience to set eyes on someone who so exactly resembled him. He wondered if he too would find the resemblance as striking as his three friends had. People sometimes didn't, he reflected. There were two men at the Savernake Club who were so alike that other members occasionally confused them: but neither of them could see it and got very angry if it were commented on.

After sitting there for a quarter of an hour without noticing a soul who could possibly be mistaken for himself, he saw Ed Travers and waved him over.

"Hullo, Jim?" the other greeted a little doubtfully, then: "Our friend turned up yet?"

"Not that I've been able to see. But, like beauty, likenesses may be all in the eye of the beholder, and I'm a biased one."

"You couldn't help spotting *this* likeness. "Why, when you waved just now, I wasn't really certain whether it was him or you."

"Sit down here and we'll watch a little longer. After all, you oughtn't to start up a game with me right away. He's the chap you really asked."

"That's true," grunted Travers and lowered his heavy body into a chair.

After a further ten minutes they decided that the stranger was not going to put in an appearance. Travers was quite disappointed. "I really did want to get you two together," he said as they at last rose for their game. "If only to convince you that I wasn't such a fool as you must think me for spending half an hour with the fellow under the impression he was you."

But Pelham was now feeling rather unhappy about it, and his game suffered in consequence.

41

"That makes me four up," remarked Travers complacently, holing out on the eighth green. "You are a rabbit today."

"Sorry, old man. But I can't get my mind off that chap. Why didn't he come after all?"

"If your theory's correct and he accepted in the hopes of remembering who I was before this afternoon, I'd say that he's realised the truth."

"How do you mean, the truth?"

"Don't be dense, Jim! Not having been able to remember me, he's come to the correct conclusion; merely that I'd mistaken him for someone else. So he's just let the whole thing drop."

"But he should have let you know."

"You certainly aren't bright today. How could he? He doesn't know my name. All he knows is this club, and how on earth could he leave a message for me by merely describing me?"

"He could have…"

"Keep quiet, old man. I'm going to drive. That foursome behind us is already coming on the green."

He drove off, slicing badly. "There! That's really your fault," he grumbled. "Making me think about strangers in pubs instead of concentrating on the game."

"I was only going to say he could have gone back to Broad's wine bar and found out who you were. It must have been obvious you were a fairly regular customer. I can see now the simplest thing for him to do was to fade away and leave you to sort it all out. After all, it was your mistake in the first place." He tee-ed up and made a beautiful drive. He was feeling better now that the matter had been satisfactorily solved, and won that hole and the next.

After the thirteenth hole Pelham was only one down. It was Travers's game that now seemed to be suffering, and the reason for it was explained when, after desultory conversation, he reverted to the subject as they walked to the fourteenth tee.

"It's all very fine, Jim, for you to say that it was my mistake, but, dammit all, anyone would have been taken in. You couldn't believe it unless you'd seen him."

"But—look at me, now, and cast your mind back—wasn't there *some* difference? There *must* have been."

Travers stopped and surveyed his companion minutely. "Hair... Moustache... Nose... Ears... Yes, all the same. Same height. And frankly I still can't see any difference in the voice, as I remember it. He was dressed like you normally are at the office, too."

"What about an umbrella?" Pelham asked suddenly. "That's an unusual habit of mine, I'm told. Wet or fine I always carry one. And Monday was a fine evening."

"Yes, but it'd been raining during the day, so he quite naturally had one. Even if he hadn't, I'd only have assumed that for once you'd forgotten. Can't you understand that right from the start I had no idea it *wasn't* you. Why, identical twins couldn't have been more alike... Here! Come on! Your drive!"

"Another thing comes to me," continued Travers a little later. "You said he must have thought I was an acquaintance he couldn't place. Well, even though we only talked about general things that wasn't my impression at the time. He spoke throughout as though he knew me well, as if it had been you and I chatting."

"But he thought then he *did* know you, just couldn't place you."

"Also he seemed to be quite familiar with Broad's, as you are."

"Maybe you only imagined that. Otherwise you'd surely have run into him there before."

"True. Still, what I mean is that it was all those points which prevented me from giving his real identity a second thought."

"I see," admitted Pelham, again vaguely unhappy about it all.

"And yet another. I've just remembered I never mentioned Oxmoor Golf Club to him by name. I thought I had, when first telling you about it, but now I recall that all I said was, 'Let's meet at the golf club at two-fifteen', as I would to you. You wouldn't have asked which one, and neither did he. So naturally I... Wait! That's funny. Surely if he thought he was being invited as a guest to my club, he'd have asked..."

"But he couldn't without giving away he'd forgotten for the moment who you... Here, I've got it of course! He assumed at any rate you were members of the same golf club, and even if he failed to remember you

43

before today, he'd recognise you when he got there. But his club *isn't* the same, and that's why he's not here."

Travers pondered, gave it up. "Oh well, it's extraordinarily confusing, whichever way you look at it."

They played on in silence for a while. Then Pelham said: "You know, the whole thing has got me. Admitted that a person can have what you'd call an absolute double, it's pretty heavy odds against them both living in London, and even heavier against them both happening to use the same part of it. And surely, they'd be detected in conversation? They wouldn't have the same background or interests, or talk about the same things."

"Yes, I think I agree. Then there's only one thing that might—I just say *might*—explain the other evening."

"What's that?" Pelham clutched eagerly at the straw. "Mac and your other friend were, understandably, cut by him. He didn't know them. But I actually called him over, and he played up."

"Seems a pointless thing to do."

"No. See what I mean. He might have been pretending to be you on purpose. He may have seen you in the street on one or two occasions, realised the likeness and then copied your dress and so on—just for fun. That would account for everything being so exactly like when I met him."

"But why should he play up to you, as you call it, wilfully deceive a friend of mine? Dammit, if you hadn't written me, I wouldn't have been out here, and you'd have thought pretty badly of me."

"That's true."

"Then why do a thing like that?"

"Oh, maybe a sort of hoax or something, I don't know."

"A hoax!" Pelham was deeply offended. "I've always been on the best of terms with everyone. No one would play that kind of trick on me."

"Not anyone who knew you. But he doesn't. Just a warped sense of humour. There *are* people like that…"

Loud cries of "Fore!" interrupted them.

"Here! We're holding people up. Whose drive is it? I've forgotten. All this blasted talk!"

They finished playing without referring to the matter again. Once more Pelham was quite off his game and Travers won by four up and two to play.

"Don't worry about the thing, Jim!" he said kindly, as they had tea together in the clubhouse. "It's not worth it. Just a flash in the pan—he's probably feeling ashamed of himself."

"Yes, I suppose that's the way to look at it."

"Maybe you'll run into him yourself one day." He laughed. "If so, bring him out here to golf and startle all the nineteenth-holers. It'll probably put half of them on the wagon for life!"

Pelham also laughed, genuinely taken with the idea. It would be a real little quip. His good humour gradually returned.

For the next two days, as he went about his daily affairs, he kept his eyes open, hoping to see the stranger for himself. What he'd do if he did, he hadn't made up his mind. His normal impulse would have been to be friendly: "Excuse me, sir. You probably observe our likeness to each other…" If he proved to be a decent sort of fellow—and gave some reasonable explanation of the incident at Broad's—it might even be amusing, as Ed Travers had suggested, to take him to Oxmoor for a game of golf, or to the Savernake for lunch. On the other hand, if it turned out that the deception had been deliberate, that was quite a different matter. Even if he'd only done it on the spur of the moment, never dreaming how it had so nearly involved Pelham in a misunderstanding with a friend, he'd have to be told firmly it was in very poor taste and that Mr J. M. Pelham would seek legal redress if he repeated his behaviour; for, since the other's movements and habits seemed to coincide with his own at several points, the same situation might easily arise again.

But though he scanned faces everywhere, he drew a complete blank and gradually ceased to bother, till by the following Friday he had once more almost forgotten the whole business. Reminded of it, however, that evening, by coming upon Ed Travers's original letter as he was squaring up his desk before leaving the office, it dawned upon him that eleven days had now passed since that peculiar encounter at Broad's, and that the obvious inference, and a most comforting one, was that the stranger had only been in the neighbourhood for a brief time and had now gone back to wherever it was he had come from some few weeks before.

He was so pleased at this conclusion that he whistled a few light-hearted bars and laughed out loud at the surprise on Lily's face as at that moment she happened to come out of her room, ready to go home.

"Ah, Miss Clement! We leave together for once. Allow me to escort you down these dangerous stairs!"

"You seem in high spirits this evening," she remarked as they descended.

"Why not? Doesn't June begin tomorrow? The best month of the year."

They were now in the street, and automatically Pelham raised his umbrella for a taxi; then wished he hadn't done so. It'd look rude his climbing in leaving Miss Clement there and yet he was somehow a little shy of offering her a lift. In his extremely conventional mind there lurked the idea that it might be misconstrued. He recalled the very forward blonde who'd been her substitute for that week.

She'd have jumped at it, no doubt—Pelham shuddered—expected to be taken somewhere for cocktails, or even kissed, or more probably both. But Miss Clement was different; only—supposing some of his office staff came out, just as they were getting in.

"Which way do you go?" he asked, hedging.

Lily smiled to herself, guessing his thoughts. If he asked her, she reflected, it would be quite a sign of life. From him, that was: most other employers wouldn't have thought twice about it. She did wish he'd conform a little more to the accepted pattern. On the other hand their intimate little talk of the previous week, the patting of her shoulder and the compliment about pretty girls had been quite promising. Maybe the proper employer-secretary relationship was taking shape at last.

"I walk to Leicester Square tube," she answered demurely, "when it's fine. Sometimes I meet my young man at the top of the street, if he's waiting there."

"Oh, Jack Benton. I remember. Is he there tonight?"

46

She was fairly certain he'd be there and in any event was going to wait for him in case, but could not resist replying doubtfully: "I couldn't say. It's not a regular appointment." Amusedly she then watched Pelham turning over the implications of this in his mind.

A taxi came up. He laid his hand on the door, cleared his throat, and said: "I'm off to my Club. I—er—can give you a lift as far as Green Park tube, if that's any help?"

Lily felt quite a little glow of triumph. "It's very nice of you, but I don't think I will. Just in case Jack's there. Many thanks all the same." She smiled at him very prettily and walked off. Yes, he was coming along quite a bit after all, she thought to herself.

Jack Benton, as she had expected, was waiting, had in fact seen her and Pelham farther down the street. He had also seen the brief conversation and Lily's smile.

"What was all that about?" he demanded a little petulantly, taking her arm. Being very much in love with her, he was inclined to be jealous.

Lily explained, but he didn't see the humorous side of it.

"What's he want to go taking you taxi rides for at all? It's not proper."

"He was going to his Club, not taking me rides, darling."

"A taxi on a fine evening like this!"

"He always does. Did you see he was carrying an umbrella? Well, rain or fine, he always does that, too." She squeezed his arm. "Don't be a silly old dear. Where are we going?"

"I don't think it's proper for employers to take advantage of…"

"Oh, don't bother about stuffy old Mr Pelham! I'm hungry. Let's go to the Strand Corner House and have bacon and eggs."

"O.K. But I do feel…" Apparently, he was about to say something further about Mr Pelham, but thought better of it. "And let's walk on the Embankment afterwards. I've got something important to tell you."

Lily's heart gave a sudden jump. She sensed intuitively what it was. But as they leaned on the Embankment wall looking out over the Thames, its full tide reflecting the looped lights of the South Bank, Jack took a long time to say the only thing she wanted to hear. In fact he began, rather importantly, about his work with Rogers and Holbrook over the last year, much of which she'd heard before. As confidential clerk, he told her, he was being entrusted more and more with valuable secrets—secrets, he hinted, almost pompously, a good many firms would give their ears to know.

"So obviously they think pretty highly of my reliability. And then today, Mr Holbrook had me in and actually asked me to sit down and have a cigarette, and then told me how pleased he was with me." Lily's thoughts were beginning to wander. Had her intuition been wrong? She loved hearing him talk about his work, but she had hoped that his interview with his employer wasn't after all the only thing they'd come down here to discuss.

"So *that's* the something important," she threw out as enthusiastically as she could.

"No, there's something more." The words came out in a rush. "Mr Holbrook hinted very definitely at a rise in salary next summer and—and I want you to marry me, darling Lily. I'm sick and tired of living without you. I didn't—I couldn't ask you before because I couldn't support you, not properly, but now I'm sure we could manage, and you know how I love you…" He did not finish the sentence because they were in one another's arms.

Some minutes passed—minutes which were for Lily sheer bliss. At last her life was complete—well, only just beginning really, but complete in one way, in that the happy future was now there, real and shining, ready to be grasped, a future too in which she would be at last safe from herself.

"We don't want to wait long, do we?" Jack asked finally.

"Oh *no*," Lily managed to get out.

She found she was half sobbing in her relief and happiness.

"Summer, Mr Holbrook said. Probably he means about July. That's two months to fix things up, look for a home, buy furniture and so on." He had all at once become very practical. "With what I've got saved in the bank…"

"Darling, don't think so much about the money. I can always keep on at the office and help out that way."

"I don't want you to," he replied firmly.

"Because you think Mr Pelham is going to take me for taxi rides?" she suggested wickedly.

"Of course not." But Lily had noticed his faint hesitation. "It's because I want to give you everything myself, on my own—and of the best."

A little cloud dimmed Lily's radiant mood. She really liked the work at Pelham Lake. Then Jack's arms were round her again.

After about ten minutes during which nothing of real importance was said, he released her. "We must celebrate this," he laughed, and walked her masterfully up Villiers Street into the Charing Cross Hotel and into an unexpected cocktail bar on the first floor, Lily much impressed that he even knew the place. Here Jack ordered brown sherry—"the best you've got."

"The drinks are frightfully expensive here," whispered Lily after they had toasted one another.

"Nothing's too expensive for me to give you," he said proudly. It was as though, once he had taken the plunge, he owned all the money in the world.

As if to demonstrate this, three-quarters of an hour later they were looking in at the barred but lighted windows of a large jewellers' near Piccadilly Circus. They were what Jack called "getting an idea of the sort of engagement ring you'd like."

Secure in the knowledge that the shop was shut for the night and that anyway Jack could never afford to patronise such an establishment, Lily entered into the game, and soon lost her heart to a square-cut emerald.

"That's absolutely lovely, that one. Emeralds are my favourite stone."

"Like it?"

"I adore it. Well, not really," she added hastily, trying to decipher the price ticket which was not clearly legible but seemed to indicate a fantastic sum, "because it's obviously right out of our class, but, as you said, just as a sort of guide." She tugged suddenly at his arm. "Come along, darling! We mustn't do too much make-believe or we'll never get back to earth again."

"There's going to be no more earth for me. I've got you and you're my Heaven."

"Darling, you are sweet!" breathed Lily, accepting it as the most poetic sentiment in the world instead of something like a line from a radio crooner's song. "I do love you. But at the moment, your Heaven's overexcited and tired and wants to be escorted to her tube station and kissed goodnight. She's got to work tomorrow just as if it were an ordinary day... Poor Mr Pelham!" She broke off. "He'll be upset by this. He relies on me rather a lot."

"He'll find someone else. Your leaving won't be a disaster. From what you tell me, he slips pretty easily through life."

"And so he ought," retorted Lily warmly. "Because he's sweet and kind and always in good spirits."

Mr Pelham, however, at that moment was in anything but good spirits. In fact, he was extremely worried, and had been so ever since first entering the Savernake Club earlier in the evening, his mind on a game of billiards.

The hall-porter had called out to him and, on Pelham's going over, had said in the benevolent manner of one reproving a careless child: "Your cigarettes, sir, I understand." And had offered him a nearly full box of fifty cigarettes.

Pelham smiled and shook his head. "Not guilty, Gough! Pity to have to be honest, but there it is."

"But surely, they're yours, sir? Paddy, the billiard-marker told me so when he handed them in. He said you forgot to take them with you after your game."

Pelham took them and looked at them closely. "They're the brand I smoke, certainly."

"That's partly how Paddy knew, sir. But he also said he was certain he saw you bring them into the billiard room with you after dinner."

"After dinner?" Pelham was all at sea.

"Yes, sir. It must have escaped your memory." Privately Gough was thinking Mr Pelham was lucky to get them back; but no doubt Paddy had considered it wasn't worth risking. A wrong decision, it seemed, for the other was staring at them as if he'd never seen them before.

"Well, perhaps they are mine," he admitted at last. "But I have no recollection of leaving them. It must have been a long time ago."

The hall-porter looked quite startled for a moment. "Long ago, sir? Why, it was only last night!"

Pelham gazed at him unseeingly for half a minute. Then without further word he moved slowly to a chair in the hall and sat down.

Billiards—dinner—last night! He hadn't been near the Club for three days.

7

S lowly as he sat there he began to grow angry. It looked exactly as though this blasted double of his was suddenly cropping up once more, just when he'd come to the conclusion he must have left the neighbourhood. But no; it *couldn't* be. Not in his own Club. The other probably didn't even know he belonged to the Savernake; and, if he had, would never have dared go there. There must be some other explanation. He stared fixedly at the cigarettes he still held, as if to drag the truth out of their inanimate substance into the living cells of his brain.

One thing he knew for certain was that he hadn't been in the Club himself. Perhaps then another member had left the cigarettes in the billiard-room; and, being the same brand that Pelham smoked, Paddy, who was Irish and therefore a bit vague and inconsequent, had got it into his head it was Pelham who had forgotten them on some other occasion. But then Paddy had further stated he was certain he'd seen Pelham bring them in. Vague he might be, but not to the extent of thinking Pelham had played a whole game of billiards when he'd never even entered the room.

Besides, Gough also was convinced he had been in the Club, and the Savernake hall-porter was famed for keeping an almost miraculous mental record of members going in and out. He was very proud of this accomplishment, being reported to have said once, "If I didn't *see* Sir John come into the Club, then he's not *in* the Club." If Gough had not firmly believed him to have been in that evening, he would have at once queried Paddy's reporting of the incident to him as occurring last night.

Still, there was just a chance Gough had slipped up for once, and Pelham waited there hopefully under his eye, in case it might jog the other's memory and he'd come over and say something like: "Thinking it over, sir, I recall you weren't in last night, so Paddy must have made a mistake." But Gough continued serenely at his job, greeting incoming members, phoning, snapping his fingers for a page, and so on.

Pelham was forced back to the conclusion that somehow or other it must have been his double after all. But the Savernake wasn't Broad's—a public place into which anyone might happen to go. He now began to wonder—though he didn't like the thought of this at all—whether he might not have been taken in deliberately.

Perhaps Ed Travers, who though not in the Savernake himself knew several members well, had happened, while in the company of one of them, to encounter Pelham's double again. After no doubt sorting out the golfing mix-up, having a laugh over it, and pointing out how funny it would have been if the other had turned up at Oxmoor after all, it had occurred to Ed to initiate a joke along those very lines. He might well have suggested, for instance, to the Savernake member that he should invite their new acquaintance to the Club one evening and pull the members' legs. If, as was quite possible, they were all three by then having a cheery drink together, it would have seemed to them no more than an excellent bit of fun.

This certainly offered a solution of the mystery, but it left Pelham feeling both angry and hurt. He just couldn't believe that anyone would have done such a thing without taking him, as the person chiefly concerned, into their confidence, would have so inconsiderately left him to find out about it for himself afterwards. All the same he'd better sound Gough out on the possibility. Neither the hall-porter nor Paddy, who knew him even better, would have been really hoodwinked; they'd certainly have been let into the secret, though it was extremely impertinent of Gough to have carried the joke on to the extent of giving him those cigarettes.

He got up and approached the man, smiling knowingly. "You know, I don't think these cigarettes really are mine, Gough. I smell a rat."

"A rat, sir?" The other's face did not, as he expected, break into a smile of the "so you've guessed" variety.

"I suspect some sort of leg-pull," he went on hopefully, wondering if he could now say outright that he hadn't been in the Club? No, not to Gough who, though Pelham could scarcely credit it—his attention must have been badly wandering at the time—had obviously been deceived after all; for the latter was now saying, "But what sort of leg-pull, sir? Paddy merely returned the cigarettes you overlooked last night."

"Oh, some joke perhaps of Paddy's," Pelham hazarded further. "You know his Irish blood. Put up to it by a member, of course."

Gough, still puzzled, replied severely: "The Club servants would never lend themselves to a leg-pull, Mr Pelham, even if suggested by a member. And certainly not in your case, sir," he added, with a sudden kindly smile, for which Pelham was deeply grateful.

"Oh well, let's forget it," he replied and putting the cigarettes in his pocket went into the smoking room.

Trying to read a paper his mind kept reverting to the whole unhappy business. He was quite convinced now that the joke explanation was too far-fetched to be true. Travers, after all, was an old friend, would certainly have told him about it first thing next morning; indeed he would more likely have insisted that Pelham should accompany them as being much greater fun. The solid fact then remained, that he had been impersonated. But actually in his own Club—that was what he couldn't get over. "It *can't* be possible," he suddenly muttered.

"Eh? Eh, what's that!" An old member, half-dozing in a neighbouring chair, thought he was being addressed.

"Nothing, General. Just talking aloud."

"What d'ye say? Oh, talking aloud. Bad habit! Wait till you're my age."

"As a matter of fact I was wondering if it were possible to have a double who..."

"Good idea! Just thinking the same meself. But only a small one for me... Here! Tandy! Large and small whisky!"

Hesitating between trying to explain that he wasn't referring to drink and that he'd rather not have whisky anyway, he found the glass in front of him. "Actually, I didn't mean that," he said in some embarrassment.

"Never mind," twinkled the General. "You've got it. It's on me, of course. What *did* ye mean then?" he asked later as they drank.

"Whether it was possible for a member to be impersonated in his own Club."

54

"Fella'd have to be extraordinary like to start with."

Pelham didn't think the other was going to be very helpful, but said politely, "That goes without saying. We'll assume they're as alike as two peas."

"Well, naturally it *could* happen. Those few members I don't know from Adam might be taken in by someone who looked like me—God help him!—but certainly not the fellas who know me."

"Meaning some members might be, but most wouldn't?"

"Exactly. Nor, fr'instance, would Tandy there, the waiter. He brings me drinks every day of me life. Nor the other Club servants. They know us better than we know ourselves. And," continued the General, swivelling round and fixing Pelham with a slightly bloodshot eye, "what would he want to impersonate a member of this Club *for*? Damned stuffy lot, most of 'em."

"That's just what I'm wondering," replied Pelham incautiously, but his companion, in full spate, had not heard. "What for, I ask you? The fun of it? Money? Pinch the chambermaids' bottoms without getting the blame? Eh? Tell me that!"

Pelham sat up suddenly. Money! The other had been helpful after all. "Oh, I don't know," he replied, anxious to get away. He finished his drink. Though he rarely took whisky he felt much better for that large and unintended one. "Have the other half?"

"No, thanks. Doing well with this."

Pelham left him and went straight up to the secretary's office on the second floor. Here, luckily, he caught Miss Butser, the assistant secretary, just finishing up.

"Evening, Miss Butser. You're late getting away, aren't you?"

"I'm always late," she said resignedly. "Was there something?"

"I can't remember whether I paid my dinner bill last night. Also"— a little touch of anxiety came into his voice—"did I cash a cheque? If I did, I forgot to make a note of it, and I'd like…"

But she was already flipping through the pages of an account book and said definitely, "No cheque yesterday, Mr Pelham."

He sighed thankfully, then realised that his fears in that direction were quite unfounded, as it would hardly have been likely that the stranger could have forged his signature accurately.

Miss Butser was now riffling through bills on a file. "And your dinner bill is paid up—twenty-five and six." She looked severely at him as if to say, "Too much for one person to spend on himself", and then went on: "Oh, I see that includes fifty cigarettes."

Pelham thanked her and went slowly out of the room. He just didn't know what to make of the business. This wasn't like being hailed in mistake for someone else and playing up to it. By paying a bill, which only members were allowed to do, it was quite conclusive that the man had been deliberately passing himself off as Pelham. And with no half-measures either. Not only had he dined, he had gone boldly downstairs and played billiards. With whom, he wondered: a stranger, most likely, not one of Pelham's friends. None of it seemed remotely possible. *Someone* surely must have had doubts about it at the time, or at least would recall them if questioned.

Something the old General had said about the servants "knowing us better than we know ourselves" came back to him. Why, there was Paddy, really an old friend, and the unknown had been playing billiards...

He went straight downstairs to the billiard-room—and was quite annoyed to find Paddy not there. His night off, Pelham remembered—just when he wanted so urgently to speak to him.

"Table just free, sir," said Ted, one of the coffee-room waiters who acted as Paddy's relief.

"I'm not playing. I just came down to see Paddy about something."

"He's off tonight, sir. Friday. Anything I can do?"

"No. I particularly wanted to speak to him personally."

Seeing the other was obviously put out, Ted asked if it were very urgent.

"Yes, it is," replied Pelham unhappily, knowing he'd never sleep properly that night unless he could get further to the bottom of last evening's incident.

"Well, sir"—Ted hesitated"—"I don't know that I ought to say this, but"—he looked at the clock—"I've got a good idea where he might be at this moment."

"Home, I should imagine," answered Pelham irritably.

The other grinned. "In a manner of speaking, sir, yes. But he lives up near Lisson Grove—Marylebone way, same part as me—and Friday

56

night regular as clockwork he's in the Green Posts pub, corner of the Grove and Charters Street."

"And you mean he'll be there now?" Pelham asked eagerly.

"I'd bet on it, sir. Till eight-thirty or so when he goes home to his supper."

It couldn't be better, thought Pelham. He was dining at home and Marylebone was practically on the way. Then with the consideration for others that was typical of him he said: "I suppose he won't mind my suddenly appearing on his own doorstep, so to speak, when he's off duty?"

"Lord, no, sir," said Ted candidly. "He'll be tickled to death. Thinks a lot of you, if I may say, on account of the interest you take in his eldest boy. *You'd* more likely be the one to mind. The Green Posts is just an ordinary local, you know. But if it's really urgent…"

"I don't want club armchairs and waiters," smiled Mr Pelham. "Just a word with Paddy. Thanks very much, Ted! You've been most helpful."

That was quite a stroke of luck, thought Pelham, as his taxi whirled him northwards, feeling he could never have waited till tomorrow in his present state of bewilderment and worry.

"This the right place, sir?" asked the driver dubiously as he pulled up on a corner. The Green Posts, a small square dingy building, which obviously existed solely for the purpose of selling drink without any irrelevant nonsense about it, did not seem to match with his neat prosperous-looking fare.

"Yes, that's right," said Pelham, checking the name, Charters Street, on the side turning. He got out, paid the man off and stood for a moment surveying the place. Then he tentatively pushed open the door marked "Saloon" and looked in.

It was not very clean and smelt strongly of stale beer and cheap tobacco. There were a few tables and chairs, but the only customers, five of them, were all standing at the bar talking to the shirt-sleeved landlord. Pelham, however, took in little of this: his sole concern was whether Paddy was there. He couldn't ascertain at once; though one man was short enough to be the little Irishman, they all had their backs to him and anyway he only knew Paddy in the Club livery. He felt suddenly ill at ease.

Then the landlord, who was facing him, looked up, and, quickly taking in Pelham's appearance, automatically straightened himself and called politely, "Good evening, sir." Apparently, it was an unaccustomed greeting for him, for the others stopped talking at once and turned, except the short one who had his glass to his mouth. There was a moment's silence, not of hostility nor even of resentment, but it at once made Pelham feel that he was not very welcome in their circle, was in fact out of place—as indeed he knew he was.

Then the other man turned, and joyfully Pelham recognised the Irish billiard-marker.

Paddy's mouth fell open for a surprised second and then he exclaimed with enormous delight: "Why, Mr Pelham, sorr!" He advanced and shook hands enthusiastically. "If it isn't Mr Pelham!"

"Hullo, Paddy!" he replied awkwardly, wondering how to explain his presence. He could hardly say, "I just dropped in by chance"; while "I wanted to have a word with you and heard you were sometimes here", would at once give the object of his visit, which he wanted to introduce tactfully, too much importance in the other's eyes.

But Paddy, who had evidently been drinking for some while, was beyond bothering about reasons; he was concentrating on facts. "Fancy seeing you here, sorr! Isn't that lucky on my night off? What'll you be having now? It's on me, it is."

Relieved that no explanation was necessary, he said, "Thanks very much! I'll have a small bitter." It was in his mind that he and Paddy would then adjourn to a table and talk, but Paddy was too delighted with the situation to allow this.

"Joe!" he called to the landlord. "This is Mr Pelham of our Club. I've been after telling you of him many a time. The one that's so kind to my Mickey, a present every birthday and always asking after him. This is the guv'nor, sorr, Mr Joe Lewis."

Pelham found his hand being shaken by the shirt-sleeved man with evident respect, and then, after formal introductions, by the others in turn. So far from being outside their circle, as he had been made to feel a moment ago, he now seemed to be the centre of it. He was quite touched. He had always been friendly with little Paddy, and to a lesser degree with all the Club servants, but had never realised how much it had been appreciated. Paddy, he observed, was utterly blissful: obviously in his loyal but unsuspected affection, he had talked a good deal about Mr Pelham to his friends—and here, as proof, was the famous man himself. Pelham couldn't let him down and, recollecting amusedly how he had actually asked Ted whether Paddy would mind him looking in, entered into friendly conversation with the group.

For the next ten minutes he completely forgot what he had come for, found himself buying drinks all round and learnedly discussing cricket.

Then he realised that if he wasn't careful, he might easily spend all evening in this novel but enjoyable atmosphere. He had to get Paddy by himself.

"Do you mind if I sit down?" he said, and in a few minutes, the others tactfully perceiving his intention, was alone at a table with the little Irishman.

Paddy was quite overwhelmed. "Me and you, sorr, sitting together like this! And fancy seeing you here at all," he repeated for about the third time. "Why, when I turned round and saw you in that doorway, I thought it must be your double now, indeed I did."

Pelham started. Paddy could not have made a more unfortunate remark, but he redeemed it by giving just the opening the other was looking for. "By the way, sorr, did you get your cigarettes?"

"Oh, oh yes. Thank you very much. I didn't know I'd left them. I thought they might have been taken accidentally by—by..." He put his hand artistically to his head. "Dear me! I can't remember for the moment who I was playing against."

"Why, Major Bellamy of course. You and him are always the boyos for getting at each other's throats with the billiards game."

So it was Bellamy, was it, thought Pelham, with whom the stranger had played? Bellamy, who also knew him quite intimately. Had he too been deceived? Paddy certainly seemed to have been, so probably Bellamy had as well. The thing was fantastic.

Feeling very subtle he inquired: "Did the Major think I was my usual self?"

"He did not, sorr." Ah, thought Pelham triumphantly; but was instantly dashed. "But for why? Because you beat him badly and he reckons you and him run about level. Very put out he was."

Pelham forced a laugh, then tried a more direct line. He produced a pound note and said seriously, "Paddy! Here's a present for Mickey. No, don't thank me. I want to ask you something important. There's a fellow very like me going about in London and—and I've got an idea he might be pretending to be me at times." He waited a moment to let Paddy's indignation subside. "Would it be possible do you think for him to come to the Club and play billiards and no one realise it wasn't me?"

"But I should be recognizing the rascal at once. Mistake anyone for *you*, sorr, is it, after all the…"

"But if this chap came down with Major Bellamy for a game, just as I so often do, you might take it for granted."

"What about the Major then? He couldn't be fooled." But he certainly had been, thought Pelham wryly. "Nor me, I tell you, not even if you were with the Prime Minister himself," he added sturdily, someone missing the logic.

"If it was someone *very* like me indeed, you might both be deceived?"

Paddy scratched his head. "If you put it like that now it might, if I wasn't paying attention." A thought came to him. "But not last night."

"Why not?"

"Because you made your joke about the cannon."

"I—I—what?" Pelham had once made a spectacularly humorous cannon in which a hard-struck ball had missed, spun from the cushion, missed again, rebounded once more and finally came to rest just touching, to his opponent's enormous indignation. Pelham had been inspired to one of his little quips and, "Third time lucky" had become a catchword between him and Paddy when some similar sort of fluke occurred in a game. "What little joke?" he went on in a hoarse voice. "Not…"

"Yes. Old 'third time lucky', sorr, of course. No one but yourself now could have said that."

"But not last night? Not last night?" he repeated urgently.

"But for certain, sorr! Surely you remember?"

"Yes, yes, I remember now," mumbled Pelham and got hastily to his feet, stammering something about not realising how late it was. With mechanical good-byes he took a dazed departure, found a cruising taxi outside and fell miserably back into the seat, his brain in a whirl. There was no doubt in his mind now that he had been impersonated at the Club last night so perfectly that everybody, Gough, Bellamy, even Paddy, had been taken in. But most frightening of all was the joke about the cannon. "Third time lucky" as far as he knew was entirely a thing between him and Paddy. He did not see how any outsider could possibly have known of it.

8

Not surprisingly Pelham had a bad night, turning back and forth in his bed till 1 a.m. when he took some aspirin and dropped into exhausted sleep.

Rogerson was so perturbed at his appearance next morning that he commented on it, adding: "As a matter of fact, sir, I didn't think you looked too well at dinner last night either."

"Probably only a bout of flu," said Pelham vaguely, his brain still churning over the extraordinary incident of Thursday night. Gough, Bellamy, Paddy—*and* that little quip about the cannon, so peculiarly his own—he could almost believe that he must have been at the Club after all and forgotten everything about it.

"Shouldn't you stay at home today, sir?" Rogerson was asking.

"No, I'd better carry on. Wait a bit! It's Saturday, of course. That's different." He sometimes didn't go to the office at all on Saturday mornings and Miss Clement only expected him when she saw him. On the spur of the moment he decided to get out of his present surroundings for a bit and try to come to grips with the problem.

"I'll go to the golf club for the weekend," he told Rogerson. "That ought to see me right."

"If you think it wise, sir."

"Why not? Lovely weather. Better than moping here. I'll change and go right away. You ring up the Dormy House and see if they've got a room: if not try the local inn—you know the one."

"Very good, sir." Rogerson was a trifle startled. He'd never known his employer make such a sudden decision. A weekend at Oxmoor was generally arranged about a fortnight ahead.

Pelham returned to London late on Sunday night in slightly better spirits. He'd played a lot of golf and had had time to do a lot of thinking. He'd had a pretty bad shock, he realised, but, serious though the matter was in every way, it did not now seem quite so inexplicably mysterious as it had been when he'd first learned of the joke about the cannon. Even that *could*, he thought, be explained—though the explanation was far from reassuring.

His reasoning had gone on the following lines. Having stumbled on the extraordinary physical similarity between them, the unknown had, as Ed Travers had suggested, taken to copying his clothes for fun. But he hadn't stopped there: for some mad reason of his own he had apparently decided to make himself even more like in every way, and had set himself to find out as much more about his quarry as possible, his mannerisms, his habits, his movements—regular enough in all conscience, Pelham admitted—what places he frequented, who his friends were, and so on. Engaged on this, he had, either by accident, or possibly even design, run into Travers at Broad's. The result had been so successful from his point of view that he had determined to go even further with the game—if such outrageous behaviour could possibly be so called. He would by then of course have found out what Pelham's Club was, and it would have been quite easy for him to encounter one of the members accidentally just outside at a time when he knew Pelham was somewhere else, and on being "recognised" accompany him in.

Once having made himself familiar with the Club, the fellow would next have tried a visit or two on his own. He could have gone to the billiard-room and there might have happened on the little joke about the cannon. Though it was basically a matter between him and Paddy, dozens of people must have heard him make it, and he had no means of knowing what was said in his absence. Especially—he was getting quite confused—when he was supposed to be present. Someone up at the table might easily have called out: "Aha! 'Third time lucky,' Pell, if I may borrow from you for a moment," or something like that; and it would have been enough for the stranger, watching for just such crumbs.

Yes, that must have been it, he came to the final conclusion, but his original bewilderment had only been replaced by worry at the present situation. For indeed it was more than upsetting to realise that someone was going about among his friends pretending to be him, and that he had no idea how to stop it. His mind kept returning to the problem all Monday at intervals during his work at the office, so that he was quite morose and absent-minded, and Lily Clement took him to task for having come to work at all: "I had a whole week off with my flu, and you've only had a weekend," she pointed out severely.

Pelham wanted to say it hadn't been flu, but as he couldn't tell her what it was, he kept silent. He couldn't tell anyone yet: he'd only be made fun of; or, if believed, might involve himself in situations where his own friends mistakenly accused him of impersonation. He must have more evidence—and the only way he could see to achieve that was actually to catch the fellow out.

This idea recurring to him as he was leaving the office, he walked to Broad's to consider it more fully over a sherry. If Travers was there, he might take him into his confidence about the Savernake incident. Ed was a hard-headed type and very shrewd; and had already displayed a willingness to be helpful.

But Travers was not there and so Pelham sat alone thinking. He had no idea how to set about trapping the man: he could only hope to run into him accidentally. There was, for instance, just a chance that he might at that very moment put his head in at the door, though of course on seeing Pelham he'd be off at once: he certainly didn't want a sudden confrontation. Nor was it likely; he'd already proved himself clever enough only to go to the Club and other places when Pelham wasn't there. Yet how did he know this? He could hardly put his head in at the Savernake to have a look, and he'd never risk boldly walking into the entrance hall, when Pelham might have come in only a short while before. The obvious answer was that the other must at times watch his movements. Only when he was certain Pelham had gone to a definite place did he go to a different one.

He here had a sudden inspiration. Supposing he was being watched now; the fellow might even be lurking outside, intent on another visit to the Club and waiting to see if Pelham was going there or not. The idea was quite absurd, he reflected angrily—a grown man spending his time watching, lurking, all for such a senseless and disagreeable reason—but the situation was fantastic enough anyhow. But— supposing he *was* watching....

Abruptly he made up his mind. He left Broad's, hailed a taxi and gave the Clitheroe Court address in a loud voice.

At Marble Arch he put his plan into operation. He stopped the taxi, paid it off and went into a telephone booth in the tube station. He was going to tell Rogerson he wasn't dining at home after all. The man would be very annoyed, he realised, but Pelham couldn't help that. This was much more important than Rogerson's feelings. Then he would take another taxi to the Savernake, spend the evening there—and see what happened.

He felt quite excited as he dialled. By the time he went to bed the whole annoying business might be over and done with.

Rogerson's suave voice was in his ear announcing the number.

"Oh, Rogerson! This is Mr Pelham here. I'm really very sorry, but I find I shan't be…"

"This is the manservant, sir," Rogerson interrupted. "What name shall I say?"

"What *do* you mean?" asked Pelham in amazement.

"I said 'What name shall I say', sir?" repeated Roger in a louder voice.

"I know you did," snapped Pelham. "But what the hell did you say it *for*?"

"Perhaps you'd better state your business?" Rogerson's voice was all at once chilly: Pelham hardly recognised it. With difficulty, he restrained an angry rebuke.

"I don't think you've quite gathered." Very clearly, he enunciated: "Listen, Rogerson! This is Mr Pelham speaking."

The reply was puzzled but once more polite. "Yes, this is Rogerson here, sir, but I'm afraid the line is rather bad. Did you say you wished to speak to Mr Pelham? If so, may I have the name, please?"

Pelham swore. Rogerson must be drunk. Furiously he shouted: "*My* name is Pelham. This is your master speak——" He checked in mid-word. Another explanation, astounding, indeed almost impossible, had presented itself. That "What name shall I say?" and "May I have the name, please?" Why, Rogerson had been speaking throughout just as if someone had rung up *when Pelham himself was at home*. He put the receiver down as gingerly as a sleeping cat and leaned against the side of the booth. A woman outside, seeing he had finished, rapped sharply with a coin on the glass. Pelham turned, looked unseeingly at her for a moment, then suddenly sprang into action. He jerked the door open, pushed rudely past, and ran in to the street. "Taxi!" he yelled and scrambled in almost before it had stopped moving.

By the time he had reached Clitheroe Court he had calmed down a little. It *was* really quite impossible that the stranger could actually have got into his flat, have been there when he phoned. Though he had never known Rogerson even remotely the worse for drink in all these five years, he was hoping to find him so now for the sake of his own peace of mind. On the other hand, if the unknown *had* got in, he now stood a pretty good chance of catching him—and that after all was what he had set out that evening to do. He grew quite excited again.

Standing outside the door of his flat, he took out his key and drew a deep breath to compose himself. Then he let himself in very quietly, shut the door and waited. Realising after a moment that Rogerson had not heard his silent entry, he called him in a voice he hoped was calm.

"Yes, sir?" The manservant came down the passage from the kitchen and Pelham studied him keenly. He seemed completely sober. It meant that his conversation on the phone had been perfectly normal, but—Pelham suddenly had a new thought—it did not necessarily mean the intruder had actually been in the flat, which now seemed too wild to contemplate. It was far more likely that Rogerson had merely thought Pelham was in when he wasn't. But then the man should have showed some surprise on seeing him come in now. It didn't make much sense. "Yes, sir?" repeated Rogerson.

"When I phoned…" He stopped hastily, began again. "By the way, I'm expecting a—a message. Has anyone phoned me?"

"Well, sir, a rather peculiar person rang up about fifteen minutes ago."

"Oh. What did he want?"

"I couldn't gather, sir. I think the line was bad at his end. There was some confusion between us, and he wouldn't give his name. Frankly, sir, he sounded a little—er—strange. I was just going to consult you when he rang off."

"Consult me? Did—did you think I was in?" He was going to add, "Don't you see I've only just arrived?" but checked himself at the look of astonishment and surprise which now definitely did appear on the other's face.

66

"Why, you were in your bedroom, sir; changing your collar and tie as usual I assumed. You hadn't been in long."

"I—I hadn't been in long," Pelham repeated. "You're certain I was in?" he pursued, still with some faint hope.

"But yes, sir. I was intending to tell you of the incident as soon as you came into the sitting-room but you left the flat again."

Left the flat again. So that explained Rogerson's lack of surprise in the first place. But perhaps it still didn't say the unknown *had* been in the flat, even though Rogerson obviously thought so.

"Did you *see* me go out?" he asked at length.

"No, sir. I was in the kitchen." Pelham relaxed in relief, then tautened again as the man continued: "But I heard you come out into the hall and the bang of the door."

"Thanks," he managed to get out, and rather dazedly entered the sitting-room. The sherry decanter was set out on a little table, but Pelham went into the dining-room and fetched the whisky. He felt he needed something stronger.

Sitting there with his drink he tried to work out what had happened, feeling almost as though he were outside the story, that this wasn't happening to him.

So the unknown *had* been there. And he couldn't have been spying on him outside Broad's, as he had been suspecting, or he'd have assumed Pelham was returning to the flat and would never have gone there himself. Besides, he was already *at* the flat when Pelham phoned from Marble Arch only ten minutes after leaving the wine bar. And he certainly couldn't have known that Pelham was secretly intending to go to the Club. It looked, he thought a little more hopefully, as if the other's private information service was capable of slipping up, in which case it mightn't be long before he was caught out. Indeed, he very nearly had been. He must have overheard Rogerson on the telephone, guessed that Pelham was wise to his being there, and slipped out quickly. Thus when Pelham turned up in person, Rogerson thought he had merely been out for a short walk.

But—and here was where Pelham shook his head in hopeless bewilderment—he just couldn't believe that Rogerson had been deceived. The other people, even Paddy, possibly, but not the man who'd been in such close contact with him all these years. True, Rogerson hadn't seen the fellow go out, but he must have admitted him in the first place; for he couldn't have got in, except by ringing the bell, with of course some story of having left his key behind. How *could* Rogerson of all people have been so taken in? He wondered just what had happened exactly and, hearing the other moving about the dining-room, he called him in.

"How did that… I mean, when you let me in…" Not for the first time, he realised how carefully he must word his inquiries when he alone knew his double's movements. "Never mind!" he went on hastily. "I just wanted to tell you I'll have dinner as soon as you can get it. I'm taking an early bed—not quite up to the mark."

"I'm sorry, sir. I'll hurry things up."

Extremely casually, Pelham continued: "Didn't *you* think I looked a little off colour when I first came in?"

"Frankly, sir, it seemed to me the moment I saw you in the hall that you appeared extremely fit. But of course the encounter was brief. Having been slightly delayed in the kitchen, I was still in the passage and you had, as you may remember, already hung up your hat and umbrella and were on your way to the bedroom."

Pelham brightened at this: Rogerson hadn't seen the intruder properly. Then the full implication dawned. "The moment I saw you in the hall." He hadn't been admitted after all: he was already inside the flat.

"But I must say, sir, since you ask," Rogerson was continuing judicially, "that you certainly don't look as well as I at first thought. Indeed, I remarked it while you were speaking to me just now when you came back from your walk."

Muttering something about perhaps seeing a doctor tomorrow, Pelham jumped up and hurried into his bedroom. He could think only of one thing: the stranger had let himself in. He went at once to the little stud-box in which he kept his spare latchkey. It was safely there. But then of course it could have been put back there afterwards, though he couldn't conceive how it could have been abstracted in the first place. Or perhaps the man had picked the lock, or used a skeleton key, or whatever it was such people did.

At this thought, he went rapidly round the room checking all articles of value. Pearl studs, links, cigarette-case, the two emergency five-pound notes in a wallet in his handkerchief drawer, other small valuables—all were safely there.

He looked round the room again and then his mouth fell open. On the dressing-table lay a slightly soiled stiff white collar and, still crumpled in it, a dark tie, such as he always wore to the office. In his mind he again heard Rogerson saying: "You were in your bedroom, changing your collar and tie as usual, I assumed." It could only recently have been taken off too, for Rogerson was always tidying up. He stared at himself in the mirror. He was still wearing his stiff collar and dark tie. He went to his wardrobe. He only had three ties of that kind, all slightly dissimilar. The other two were both there: the one which lay on the dressing-table was an exact replica of that which he was wearing at the moment. He would, indeed, have sworn it was the tie he had put on that morning, the tie that he would have left lying there when he changed to a less sedate one and a soft collar—had he done so.

He continued for some while to stare at himself in the mirror, completely stupefied. What was the meaning of it all? Here was a man, already like himself in appearance, who from some strange kink or other was setting out to make himself equally like in behaviour and habits—and extremely successfully too, as the evening in the Savernake had shown. Yet, not content with that audacious effort, he had next managed to get into Pelham's flat. In neither place, however, had he done anything out of the ordinary. At the Club he did not seem to have run up any bills, or borrowed money—merely dined and played billiards just as Pelham would have done. At the flat he had taken nothing, as far as could be seen—merely gone straight to the bedroom as Pelham would have done, and changed his collar and tie, again just as Pelham would have done. It was all quite unintelligible.

He looked again at the strange dark tie, started to check the less sober ones to which he would have changed to see if one of them was missing, but he could not remember how many he should have. And anyway he was now wondering what his uninvited visitor's next move would have been if he hadn't had to slide off quickly. Was he intending to go into the sitting-room and have a glass of sherry, once more as

Pelham would have done? No, that was too absurd; it would soon have brought him into close contact with Rogerson who'd have been bound to realise his earlier mistake. Besides, he couldn't thus go on behaving as if he were the owner of the flat. He must know that Pelham would soon be returning for his dinner. Yet it was quite inconceivable that he had done all this merely to effect an exchange of collars and ties; for, as far as Pelham could make out, this seemed to have been all that had actually happened.

Oh, what *did* it all mean? Nothing seemed to make any sense. He sat abruptly on the bed, an extremely worried little man.

9

"**I**s that Miss Clement? Good morning, miss. This is Rogerson. I am speaking for Mr Pelham. He is breakfasting in bed and wishes me to say that he is not very well, and…"

"Oh dear! That flu hanging on, I suppose. I told him he should never have come to work yesterday. And out playing golf all the weekend too."

"I don't think it's entirely flu, miss. It appears to be also some sort of personal worry. He hardly spoke a word to me at dinner last night and went straight off afterwards. He's going to take it easy this morning, but says he'll look in in the afternoon."

"Tell him from me he's not to," said Lily Clement firmly. "Everything's under control here. Make him stay in bed all day, Rogerson."

"I'll try, miss," agreed Rogerson. "But he is in a somewhat difficult mood."

Poor Mr Pelham, thought Lily as she rang off, wondering what it was that was troubling him. She had thought yesterday that he'd been a little more "in the dumps" than a bout of flu warranted; indeed she had forborne to worry him further by telling him her news—it was the first time she had seen him since Jack had proposed—because it would also have meant breaking to him that she'd be leaving to get married in the summer. She knew she ought to tell him as soon as possible so that he could look round for a successor. Still a few days wouldn't make too much difference and a short spell in bed would probably see him quite fit again.

But Pelham didn't stay in bed, even for the morning. By ten o' clock he was up and about. The problem had been running round and round in his brain like a squirrel in a cage till he found it impossible to lie there any longer. He must *do* something. He couldn't have total strangers making free with his Club and his flat without taking drastic steps to stop

71

it. It was more than probable that the man was up to some nefarious purpose—though what he did not know, and the way he was going about it was quite outside Pelham's experience.

Pacing round the sitting-room he considered going to the police. But just what to tell them he hadn't an idea. He could hardly say an unknown man closely resembling him had picked the lock of his flat— for that was the only way he could have got in, Pelham had now decided—and had been there for some while, even being seen by his manservant. They'd only check up with Rogerson, and the latter was quite convinced that it was his master who'd come home in the first place and then gone out again for a short walk. That he did have a double could be proved by Camberly, MacAndrew and Travers; but that the likeness was so good as to deceive his own manservant in his own flat, even though the latter had only seen him briefly, would sound quite incredible in the prosaic atmosphere of a police station.

No, he must discuss it with someone first, see what they thought he should do, and at once Ed Travers came to his mind. He had vaguely considered confiding in him last night, and probably would have done if the other had happened to be in Broad's. This last effrontery made the other's advice imperative.

He went quickly to the telephone, rang Travers's office and asked if he'd meet him for lunch. "Something I want to discuss with you," he explained.

"Sorry, old boy. No can do. I'm going out of town this morning. Catching a train at Waterloo at eleven-thirty."

Oh," said Pelham, disconcerted. Now that he had made up his mind to tell Travers he wanted to do it as soon as possible. "When will you be back?" he asked anxiously. "This evening?"

"Lord, no, I'm away till Friday. What's it all about?"

"That infernal double of mine again."

"What?" Travers was at once interested. "Have you met him at last? Going to bring him out to golf?" he laughed.

"No, no. It's past all that, Ed. It's got really serious and I'm worried sick about it. I simply must talk it over with you."

Travers considered. He liked being asked for advice, and Pelham sounded genuinely upset. "Tell you what I'll do then, old man. I'll clear up things here quickly and meet you at Waterloo station at eleven… No, wait! Nowhere to talk properly. Go to the bar, buffet—whatever they call it—of the Air Terminal. It's just across the road. Upstairs."

Pelham thanked him gratefully and rang off, already much reassured by Travers' confident matter-of-fact voice.

At five to eleven he was at the rendezvous and a moment later Travers came bustling in carrying a suitcase. "Hm!" he said critically. "You certainly do look worried, Jim! Well, come on; let's hear all about it!" They sat down to one of the low tables at the glassed-in side of the long buffet and ordered coffee.

Pelham began by outlining briefly Friday's billiard-room incident and his meeting with Paddy and then described in more detail what had happened the night before.

Travers sat back and whistled. "Well, I said at the time that that golfing mix-up just about beat the band, but this beats the whole Albert Hall orchestra."

"What's it all *mean*?" asked Pelham desperately. "It's beyond any joke, beyond even deliberate annoyance. It's…" His voice trailed away to silence.

Travers stirred his coffee and stared thoughtfully for a minute at the airport buses arriving and departing on the broad stretch of tarmac outside.

"I think it's obvious that you're up against a really clever criminal."

Pelham nodded his reluctant agreement. "But what's he after? I've missed nothing, and one way and another he could have had quite a nice little haul in my bedroom alone."

"He's evidently out for something bigger. Just look at the trouble he's already gone to—copying your clothes, your movements, even your catchwords—all to make himself as indistinguishable from the real you as possible. But what that something… One minute! I've just thought. You've got a passport, I suppose?"

"Yes, at home. But…"

"Check up as soon as you can whether it's there. It could be extremely valuable to a man so exactly like you, who for some criminal,

73

or more probably political, reason can't get one. Everything may have led up to that."

Pelham brightened. "That's an idea."

"On second thoughts, though, I don't think he'd really have done all that he has—that visit to the Club for instance, and, as you say, probably others earlier—just for that."

"He was seeing if he could deceive Gough and Paddy and other people actually in my own surroundings, not just a place like Broad's, before he tried it on Rogerson."

"Yes, but one straightforward burglary when your chap was out would have done the trick equally well. And why the hell change his collar and tie? I'm beginning to think he's a loony."

"A pretty unusual one," snapped Pelham angrily.

"Ye-es. I don't think that's really the correct answer, either." He drank some coffee and again stared out of the window. "This getting into your flat. You think he fiddled the lock, you say. Risky thing to do with your man actually inside: no chance of pretending to be you then. Mightn't he have had a duplicate key?"

"Impossible. My spare was in my bedroom."

"It could have been borrowed and a copy made."

"Borrowed? But how could he?"

"I don't like to suggest it—forgive me, old man—but suppose your manservant..."

"I'd trust Rogerson anywhere with anything," Pelham cut in coldly. "He's absolutely dead straight. He's been with me for..."

"All right, Jim, all right. Anyway, the fellow's got a key now."

"No. My spare one was still there, I told you."

"Of course, old chap. But naturally he took a wax impression when there. In fact, maybe that's why he broke in in the first place. He now has the freedom of your flat."

"You aren't being very comforting, you know, Ed."

"I'm merely assessing the situation at the moment," replied Travers a little pompously. "I'll be more constructive in a few moments. And anyway it's just as well to know what you might be up against."

Up against, thought Pelham miserably. Why should he be up against anything! What had he done to deserve this trouble; he who always tried to be friendly to everyone?

"The more I look at it," Travers was continuing, "the more I think the chap has some really big coup in mind, and this impersonating of you here, there and everywhere is only a preliminary part of it. Now!" Pelham was about to speak but the other raised his hand. He was in the chair: the hard-headed businessman giving advice to a friend very much in need. "Now! What about bringing the police in?"

Pelham told him his views on this, ending, "You see, I've lost nothing: I've never seen this man; and everywhere he's been when he shouldn't, people will swear that it was *me*." He suddenly took from his pocket the tie that had been left on the dressing-table. "This tie is exactly the same kind, bought at the same shop, as those I wear. But I alone know it isn't mine. *He* wore it, and left it in my bedroom—God knows why. Does that really sound to you something to tell the police?"

"Frankly, no," admitted Travers. "He'll have to be allowed to go a little further before we blow police whistles. Once you can catch him out, confront him, you've got him."

"Oh, quite easy!" said Pelham sarcastically. "I've only been trying for a fortnight!"

Travers, very pleasantly conscious of the extent to which his friend was relying on him, was unruffled. "Listen!" He glanced at his watch. "And I must make it snappy or I'll miss my train. What I'd advise you to do is this. You're a chap of regular habits and dress and so forth. That's what he's relying on. Well, start varying your movements: go to places you don't usually go to, turn up at your Club at times you've never been before, get a new suit of quite a different style or pattern, and—oh, you see what I mean—drive off the old Pell tramlines and be a bus for a bit. I honestly think that in this way you may baffle the fellow and trip him up. And then you *will* have a case for the police."

Pelham nodded dubiously, a little unhappy. The other got up, put a friendly hand on his shoulder. "I don't sound very helpful to you, I can see, but it may do the trick. However clever the scoundrel is, the police will nab him, once you can give them something to go on. And he can't keep it up without a false step somewhere. It isn't humanly possible."

Pelham nodded again. "But he just doesn't seem human," he said. "Look at what he's got away with already."

"I know, I know. Well, so long! I'll be back Friday evening and will give you a ring right away. And we'll hope nothing more has happened by then—except perhaps that the chap's in jug." He picked up his suitcase and started for the exit, then came hurriedly back. "Just thought. Something important. The whole object of his campaign may have been to get into your flat and obtain your signature on documents."

"My signature?"

"For cheques, old man. And other things. Once he'd really practised up your signature, and looking the exact image of you as he does, he could do the hell of a lot." That was a fine note on which to leave a fellow, thought Pelham bitterly, but the other raced on: "If I were you, I'd change your signature—just slightly, not drastically. Tell your bank to cash no more cheques dated as from today which don't have the new one. Try it! Must fly!" And he was gone.

Pelham lit a cigarette and sat on for a while. The immediate effect of his talk was disappointment, till he reflected that he could hardly have expected the other to wave a wand and cause his unknown double to disappear into thin air. And though his summing-up of the situation had been most disturbing—he had made Pelham feel like a fly caught in a web, not knowing when or how the spider was going to pounce— he had at least given the most helpful advice he could.

He was not, however, particularly drawn to the idea of suddenly changing his various pleasant little habits; while all that stuff about wearing different clothes, altering his signature and so on, smacked too strongly of lurid detective fiction. He came to the conclusion it might be better after all to tell the police about it right away.

Thirty minutes later he found himself in Bow Street Police Station facing a stolid-looking sergeant at a desk. He began somewhat haltingly by explaining that he was being impersonated by a man who resembled him exactly and then briefly outlined the incidents at Broad's and the Savernake. "And only last night," he concluded, "he actually got into my flat in Maida Vale and passed himself off as me to my manservant. He was there for…"

The sergeant, who had listened courteously up till then now interrupted: "One moment, sir! Just what has he stolen?"

"Nothing as yet." Pelham only wished he could report that his passport had been taken. But before coming into the police station he had checked with Rogerson that it was safe in its usual place. It hadn't really been very likely that that had been the object of all the long and complicated manoeuvrings: and if it had, he would have reported the loss in writing, accepted it joyfully as ending the whole business, and never involved himself in this present difficult interview. "But," he went on awkwardly, "I feel—in fact I'm certain—he's only waiting for an opportunity to do so. Or do something else," he added lamely.

The sergeant looked thoughtfully at Pelham. He was accustomed to cranks of all sorts, imagining all kinds of things, but his visitor looked reasonably normal and respectable.

"He seems to have had opportunities already, sir. Till he is caught doing something illegal or attempting to, it's a little difficult, you understand."

"But isn't impersonating me illegal?"

The other paused, then choosing his words carefully: "From what you say he hasn't been caught doing even that yet. Unless of course your servant can state..."

"No, my servant was certain it was me. So is everyone who meets him."

The sergeant just refrained from raising his eyebrows despairingly heavenwards. "Surely, sir, actually talking to people who know you, as I gather he has done, would at once give him away."

"But it doesn't. He's... Well, he's made himself into the exact image of me." More and more he was realising the uselessness of trying to make the policeman understand. It was just as he had foreseen. He wished he had never come.

Evidently this was in the sergeant's mind too. He had only listened so long out of curiosity and a desire to be helpful if he could. He now decided privately to pass the buck.

"I'm afraid there's not much we can do. In any case, while I realise your office is in our area, the particular incident you're reporting seems

77

to have occurred at your flat in Maida Vale. I think you'd do better to go to your local station and see what they suggest."

Thanking him perfunctorily, Pelham went quickly out, relieved that it was over, and glad he hadn't produced the tie he had in his pocket. It would certainly have made the sergeant think he wasn't right in the head, whereas he'd now merely be put down as a harmless individual with a bee in his bonnet. He had finished with the police—at any rate until, as Travers had said, the unknown had gone a little further, made a false step. He could see now that no one could begin to believe his story, unless they'd actually met and talked to the fellow.

He lunched at a restaurant in Aldwych where he'd never been before. He supposed he might as well try altering his movements a bit: it seemed to offer the only chance of ultimately laying the criminal by the heels. Then he went to his bank in Fleet Street and asked to see the manager.

"I was wondering," he began, feeling rather a fool, "if I wouldn't change my signature."

"By all means, old chap; it's your property," laughed the other, a pleasant man about five years older than Pelham. They were on quite a friendly basis: indeed Carter was a member of the Oxmoor Golf Club. "Any particular reason? Or have you just got sick of it?"

Pelham accepted the excuse. "That's about it. One does, you know. Remember how as adolescents we were always trying new variations, different style of capital letters, and so on?"

"Till we were old enough to have a bank manager to make us settle down, eh? Well, let's see! You now sign 'James M. Pelham', don't you? Who do you want to be in future? Just the J.M., or the full names—Montagu, isn't it?"

"Oh, nothing very sweeping. Just a slight alteration—maybe only in the way I write one letter."

"I see," said Carter, suddenly thoughtful "Anything funny going on?"

"No," lied Pelham. "Well, not exactly. But I thought that if your clerks were all advised to look out for the new signature and accept only that…"

"Laying a trap, eh? Hadn't you better tell us? We could help, you know."

For a moment Pelham was tempted to further confidences, then thought better of it.

"If you've lost your chequebook, we'll have the numbers notified to..."

"No, it's not very much really."

"Very well. Now for the new signature! We'll want specimens."

Pelham suddenly felt tired of the whole silly business, and not a little angry. He seemed to be being forced out of his own identity. He rose to go. "I'll work out something and write you. I just wanted to put the possibility up to you first."

Carter shook hands. "You can sign yourself 'Lady Slapcabbage' if you like, as long as we have a specimen and know that it is definitely *you* giving your instructions to *us* to pay out your money. That, plus a stamp, is all a cheque is."

Leaving the bank, Pelham decided against going to the office after all. He had said that morning he would go, so this seemed just another small way of varying his movements. Instead he took a taxi to his tailor in Conduit Street and ordered a new suit.

Here he ran into trouble and was forced to realise what a creature of habit and fixed tastes he really was.

"We've cut for you, for all these years, Mr Pelham, and we know your requirements. If you insist on having a single-breasted suit for town wear, when you've always..."

"But I want something different."

"Hm! And that pattern you've selected, if I may mention it again"— the tailor was referring to a verbal skirmish of a few minutes previously—"I still say it's quite wrong for you."

Baffled, Mr Pelham once again put off a decision. "Very well, you can hold up the order; I'll think it over," he said abruptly and walked out into the street, round the corner and into the shop where he bought his hats.

Without opposition this time he bought a light brown hat of a somewhat jaunty style. He hadn't worn brown for many years, and the style was a little repugnant to him, but he was trying to follow Travers's advice.

"Do you wish to wear it, sir? We can send on the old one?"

"All right... No, send the new one. I'll take it into wear later. I—I have a new suit being made to go with it," he quibbled, wondering whether all this nonsense would really be any good. But he didn't see what else he could do to put a spoke in the unknown's wheel and prevent him going further with his plans—whatever they were. He only wished to Heaven he had some inkling. The thing was without rhyme or reason at the moment.

As a final gesture, or rather a further move in the new scheme of counter-attack, he went to the Zoo, which he hadn't visited for ages, had tea there, and actually enjoyed himself, though at intervals he was assailed by the distressing conviction that he'd spent his day like a cross between a hunted man and a schoolboy playing truant.

10

For the rest of the week, as if satisfied with having successfully impersonated Pelham in his own flat, the unknown made no further move. And Pelham himself found, as many people had done before him, that once he had confided in someone his troubles seemed lessened. No longer was he alone in a dark wood while strange, inexplicable things happened around him; he had a companion. True, it was not Ed Travers who was directly concerned, but it did make a difference.

Lily Clement was delighted to note how much better he looked, though she could see he was still by no means back to the Pelham of a month ago. Something had happened which she did not know about and which had caused him great worry, but it seemed to be sorting itself out. Meanwhile she had had a small private worry of her own to contend with. Jack had presented her a few days previously with an engagement ring which was exactly the same as the emerald one at which they had looked on that wonderful evening.

"And I bet you anything," he said, as he put it proudly on her finger, "you couldn't tell this one from the one you picked on in the shop window."

"I'm *sure* I couldn't," she replied ecstatically, turning her finger to and fro. "It's an absolutely wonderful imitation. Sorry! That somehow makes it sound cheap and nasty, when it's *beautiful!*" A sudden awful thought assailed her. "Jack! It *isn't* the same one, is it?"

"What do *you* think?" he laughed.

"Well, I know it can't be, because it would have taken all your savings, and you'd never have... But it's *exactly* like it." She admired it again, but now with slight misgiving. "Darling, do promise it isn't?"

"Ask no questions and you'll be told no lies! Remember, I have it on the best authority that it's 'the sort of ring you like'."

"But darling, you *must* tell me. I shall be horribly angry if..." She broke off. He was right; she mustn't cross-examine him, and anyway she was positive he wouldn't really have bought that very same ring, just because of their little make-believe. He was far too sensible.

All the same there had still remained in her mind the haunting suspicion, knowing Jack's devotion to her, that it *might* have been, and she even started out the next day to see if the ring they had looked at was still in the window. But before she got there, she changed her mind. She knew in her heart he couldn't have afforded it, and it didn't seem fair, when he had been so clever as to track down such a perfect replica, to spoil his little triumph even secretly. And by the following day, fairly convinced that it couldn't be the same, she decided that it would be rather thrilling and original never to know for certain. Real or not, it was a lovely stone and she adored it.

Pelham also, after warmly congratulating her on her engagement, had admired it greatly. "Your young man *is* doing you proud," he said. "It's quite charming. And is the happy day fixed?" he added a little wistfully, obviously concerned with the thought of having to replace her.

She hesitated a moment, then replied casually that nothing had been definitely settled yet. Her formal notice could wait just a little longer. Giving it, even for two months ahead, seemed so irrevocable. And, though Jack had said he didn't want her to go on working after her marriage, she was hoping he might change his mind. The extra money would certainly be a great help. Besides, her Mr Pelham was becoming so much more human, patting her shoulder, referring pointedly to "pretty girls" and offering taxi rides—in general, beginning to behave quite like a normal employer should towards his private secretary.

Ed Travers returned on the Friday evening. As he had promised, he at once rang Pelham at his flat.

"Well, Jim, I'm back. Any news?"

"Nothing to report, Ed. Not a smell of him."

That's fine." Somehow he sounded a little disappointed, Pelham thought. People were always interested in trouble, he reflected—as long as they were on the outside looking in. "But I can't stop now, old man. There's a great kerfuffle going on here—welcome home from the wife and kids, you know. It was just a friendly call to ask after our pal. Let's meet tomorrow and have a proper talk. What about golf?"

"That'll suit me nicely. Actually I wasn't thinking of going to the office tomorrow morning. Shall we make it a day?"

"Sorry, old chap! I've got a heck of a lot to do at my place after being away. I…" He broke off to tell some child who was pestering him—Pelham could hear the eager "Daddy! *Do* come!" in the receiver—to be a good girl and wait one tiny minute.

"Then two-forty-five. That O.K., Ed?"

"Fine."

They met as arranged, but decided not to play golf for half an hour or so when the crowd would have thinned out, and so settled down on a corner of the veranda.

"Do you think it's possible he's finished with his games?" asked Pelham hopefully after a few minutes' talk.

"No. I still feel he's just biding his time. What makes you think that?"

"Well, I've been wondering these last days if it mightn't all have been some sort of a wager."

"Wager? How on earth…"

"Oh, I don't know." It did sound rather far-fetched now he actually voiced it. "I mean he may have had friends who ran across me and noticed the extraordinary likeness, and betted him a large sum he couldn't actually get into my home without being caught out, and everything's just been leading up to that. After all, all he did was to take a collar and tie of mine—perhaps as proof."

"You mean he's now collected the stakes and has finished with you? Hm! I see. But I don't think it holds water, Jim. I admit that some mad young practical joker might have taken it on—you know, like the fellow once who dressed up as an Oriental potentate and got shown officially over a battleship or something, I forget now—but it's highly unlikely that the one man in the world who happens to resemble you exactly—a man of your age too, remember—would be that type. No, out of the question," he summed up.

Privately, Pelham still thought it was a possibility, but bowed to Travers's wider knowledge of the world. "Why *has* he stopped, then?"

"I told you. He's making his plans for the big killing."

"I wish you'd be a little more encouraging, Ed."

"There's no sense in shutting your eyes to facts—well, possibilities, then. By the way, have you been varying your movements and so on as I suggested when last we met?"

"A little bit," Pelham admitted guiltily. After the first two days, in fact, he hadn't gone much further with the idea. It had been more difficult than he imagined to break the routine of years. Besides, other people wouldn't let him do it. He recalled Rogerson's horror when the pale brown hat had arrived. Assuming it had been sent in error, he just wouldn't believe his master had ordered it; and when convinced that he had, had merely said, "*After* lunch, I presume, sir," in humorously ironical tones, and promptly put it away somewhere where Pelham hadn't been able to find it. Lily Clement too had been quite upset when, on the day following, he had not put in an afternoon appearance at the office till five o'clock and then told her he was going to work there alone up to seven. She had wanted to stay behind also, and there'd been quite a little fuss. "You see, Ed," he finished, "it's rather difficult for a man in my position."

"Never mind! You've been doing it. And there's no doubt," he continued complacently, "that that's what's baffled him this last week. He's had to start studying you all over again."

"But it hasn't brought me any nearer catching him apparently, and that was the main idea of your suggestion."

"It'll work out," returned Travers a little huffily. "What about your signature, by the way? For cheques," he added as Pelham looked blank.

"Oh that. I haven't actually done it, but I've spoken to my bank manager."

"Well, in your own interests I should get it going as soon as possible."

They sat in silence for a moment, Pelham rather depressed by the conversation. But Travers was right, he supposed. He'd write to Carter about his signature that weekend.

"Hullo, you two!" a friend's voice interrupted. "Care to make a foursome with Dennis and me?"

"Well," began Travers and glanced at Pelham. "Have we said all we wanted, Jim? Or can I be of any more help?"

"No, you've been most kind, Ed," he answered a little despondently. They got up and the four men went out to play.

When by ten-thirty that Saturday morning Pelham had not turned up, Lily Clement realised he was not coming at all. Ah well, she thought, it'd do him good. And anyway, nothing much happened on a Saturday morning either.

In this she was proved wrong, for at eleven-thirty she had a visitor, a M. Thiers from Paris, a dark fattish middle-aged man with rather shifty eyes.

"I'm terribly sorry," she explained, "but Mr Pelham sometimes takes Saturday morning off. He'll be in on Monday. Or I can ring him right away and find out if…"

"Ah, no, miss. Monday is well suitable." His eyes roved appreciatively up and down her figure in a way which embarrassed, yet half-flattered her. "I am here during a week, and it is just that my firm, Berthier *et Cie*, wished me to make contact with Messrs Pelham Lake, while over here."

As far as she knew, the firm was not one with whom Pelham did business but she asked him, in order to make certain.

"No, we are not associated." He smiled. "Not as yet. But we might perhaps come to be. In fact, I have a certain proposition to make."

New business, thought Lily. Why did her employer have to be away this morning?

"I'm sure Mr Pelham will be most interested." She reached for the engagement book on Pelham's desk. "May I make a definite appointment for…" At that moment, the phone rang, and with an "Excuse me", she answered it.

"Yes… Yes, it's me… Yes, there *is* something." Covering the receiver, she said: "Isn't that lucky? Mr Pelham is on the line asking if anything particular is happening in the office." Then to the phone again: "There's a M. Thiers here." Briefly she explained the situation, then told the visitor: "Mr Pelham says he can't get down here right away, but perhaps you'd be free to lunch with him, if you don't mind it being a little early. Would you like to talk to him yourself?"

"No, no matter. Tell him I shall be charmed."

The girl spoke into the phone again and then listened. At one point she gave a little start and a slow smile crossed her lips. She'd hardly been able to believe her ears: for the first time Mr Pelham had called her "Lily".

"Mr Pelham says twelve-thirty at Simpson's. I'll engage a table in his name and will you ask the head waiter to show you to it."

"But certainly."

She confirmed, laughing suddenly at something that was said and then replacing the receiver.

"He seems an amusing man," volunteered M. Thiers. I shall enjoy meeting him?"

"I think so," she smiled. "He sounds in excellent spirits today, but he hasn't been too well lately." She broke off, realising it was not her business to discuss her employer, and, after ascertaining that he knew where the restaurant was, showed her visitor out.

She returned to her own room feeling quite excited and hoping something would come of the lunch. Ever since she'd been with Pelham Lake, the only firms they'd had dealings with were those with whom they'd been associated for years. Here perhaps was a chance for Mr Pelham to branch out, be a little more go-ahead, as she'd always been quietly urging him to do. Not so quietly either, at times, she reflected, remembering her enthusiastic little homily of a fortnight ago. She suddenly wondered if that had really impressed him: he'd certainly sounded self-confident and absolutely on top of the world just now. *And* at last he had called her "Lily". Again she felt sorry that she'd probably be leaving Mr Pelham just when things seemed to be getting quite interesting.

Anyway, she fervently hoped he'd open up that Paris connexion. The French side seemed very willing or they wouldn't have sent M. Thiers along specially. It might mean his shortly going over to Paris in return. *And* he might even take his secretary. She laughed to herself. That'd give Jack something to think about.

For rather to her surprise, Jack had once again referred to the incident of Mr Pelham and the taxi, banteringly but with an undercurrent of what she could only interpret as jealousy. How could she make him see that jealousy just couldn't exist between them? She was longing for the haven of peace and satisfied happiness that marriage with him would bring, the knowledge that she would be free for ever from herself and in his care.

At twelve-thirty she left the office and made for a little restaurant in Soho. Her brother Tom was on one of his visits to London and had asked her to lunch. She was very fond of Tom; though actually a year younger than she was, he bossed her about as if she were a kid sister. She was certain that if he hadn't been away doing his Army service just at the time when she first came to London she'd never have been allowed to involve herself in that humiliating and miserably revealing affair.

He greeted her with great affection, then forcefully marched her off to a table, told her to sit down, and thrust a napkin into her hand.

"It's only revenge for what you used to do to me when I was a schoolboy," he grinned when she protested that she was not a child in rompers but a grown woman. "I'm the boss now. Besides, you haven't knocked about the world like I have."

"I'm jolly glad I haven't from what you've told me of your life."

"I've had to be tough," he admitted, rather too complacently, Lily thought. "You know, push people around a bit. Otherwise they push you."

"Oh, Tom! I wish you didn't feel like that about things."

"I can't help it. If only I could get a job that really suited me."

"I thought you liked your present one all right."

"Yes, but it's so dull. And soppy."

"Nonsense! You're making good money, and it's civilized, and you meet people and... I suppose really," she broke off thoughtfully, "you ought to have been living a couple of hundred years ago. Then you could have been a soldier of fortune and sold your sword to the highest bidder."

Tom laughed. "I might even try it now. Put an advert in the paper: For Sale. One sword, tough owner, go anywhere, do anything... Hullo! Here you are at last!" This rather masterfully to the waiter. He began characteristically to order for them both, without inquiring her preference. Lily rather liked that. It saved her the trouble of making up her mind. Kindly Mr Pelham, she felt—in the inconceivable event of him taking her out to lunch—would have spent hours asking her about every item so as to be sure she had just what she liked.

She and Tom had a hilarious lunch but afterwards, over their coffee, he suddenly turned serious. "I didn't tell you, did I, I looked Jack up just before coming here? I wanted to congratulate him in person and tell him what a lucky man he was."

"And warn him to treat me right?" she teased.

"Of course. Joking apart, Lil, I do hope the two of you will be very happy."

"I'm dead sure of it." The warm cosy feeling of security again flooded her.

"There's just one thing. Look, Lily, I don't want to butt in, but Jack seemed a little worried about—well, about you and your boss going off for taxi rides in…"

She gave a little peal of laughter. "Jack's being an absolute idiot." She related the circumstances, but all Tom said was, "Some employers think secretaries fair game. You be careful, Lily."

"Oh, you *are* old-fashioned. Do you think I can't look after myself?"

"Then you *have* had cause to…"

She struggled to maintain her good humour. "Listen, Tom. I've told you about this particular employer before. He's just naturally kind and sweet—sort of paternal. I've never been out with him even for half an hour, if that's what you're driving at. Why, up to today, he's never called me anything but Miss Clement!"

"But he doesn't any longer, you mean?"

Lily merely shrugged, her fingers irritably tapping the table at her brother's stupidity.

Tom misinterpreted her silence. "If any man starts fooling around with my sister," he burst out angrily, "he'll find she's got a brother to reckon with who…"

"Listen, Tom!" Her voice was icily sharp. "He called me 'Lily' this morning for the very first time after all these months. And in an age when practically on first acquaintance every Tom, Dick, and Harry…"

"Sorry, Lil! But it was Jack who… I mean, this Mr Pelham of yours may be playing a deep game."

"Utter nonsense!" All the same her fingers suddenly stopped tapping as she recalled that Joyce had said something of the same sort, about the simple ones being the deepest. She just couldn't imagine Mr Pelham being deep. She'd been with him eight months, and if there was anything really like that in his nature she'd have spotted it before. Or was it just that he was naturally very shy, and had been taking his time? It was rather fun to think of in a way… She checked her thoughts, which were getting a little out of control, angry with Joyce, and now with Tom for having put such absurd ideas in her head—and on the verge of a happy married life too. "I think you're being just a little too much the protective brother," she told him severely. "Now don't let's talk about it anymore, or you'll spoil the lovely meal we've had."

"All right, old girl."

Lily had a further thought. "You're in town for a few days. Come and fetch me at the office for lunch on Monday and I'll introduce you to Mr Pelham. Then you can see for yourself. And if you aren't convinced, you can chuck your car-selling job and appoint yourself my personal bodyguard."

11

Late on Sunday evening Pelham had a trunk call from Crewe. An aged and invalid aunt had died that afternoon. He and a local solicitor were her executors, and it was the latter now phoning. Could Mr Pelham find it convenient to come down next day, as there were various legal matters to discuss, as well as the arrangements for the funeral? Pelham looked briefly at his diary, found no particular engagement, and replied that he would catch the first available train on Monday.

Before leaving next morning, he emphasised to Rogerson that he'd be away all day. That, he felt, would put a spoke in the double's wheel if he tried getting into the flat again.

"Shall I inform Miss Clement later?" the man had asked. It was still too early for anyone to be at the office.

Pelham told him that he'd do that himself at Euston; he wanted to tell Lily also about his altered signature. For he had that afternoon written to Carter enclosing specimens of the change—definite but slight, merely the capital "P" differently formed—and stating that no cheques drawn either on his personal account or the firm's, or any other documents dated after the Monday and not so signed were to be considered as his. He couldn't help feeling rather foolish as he posted the letter, but reminded himself he'd look even more foolish if the unknown double had some fraudulent project in mind and he hadn't taken every possible precaution. Travers, he knew, was convinced that the other was definitely planning something, and Travers was more worldly-wise than he was. For the hundredth time Pelham wished he had some idea of what the fellow was really after. He rather regretted having to go out of town, till he reflected that Ed had urged him to vary his movements, and there could hardly be a greater variation than the unexpected death of a great-aunt sending him to Crewe at a moment's notice.

At Euston he phoned his office and was annoyed to get the engaged signal. He dialled twice more and then had to run for his train. Tuesday would do, after all, to tell Lily about the signature, and when he didn't appear at the office she'd undoubtedly ring up his flat and learn from Rogerson that he'd been called away.

He got back to London about six-thirty, and promptly rang the Savernake. It had occurred to him that the unknown might have found out about his absence and taken advantage of it. In an assumed voice he asked Gough if Mr Pelham was in the Club, rather hoping the answer would be that he was. He would go flying down there and confront him at last with plenty of witnesses. But Gough reported in the negative.

On his arrival at the office on Tuesday Lily Clement, coming in with pad and pencil as usual at his summons, welcomed him in such obviously buoyant spirits that he commented on it.

"My absence seems to have done you good," he remarked humorously. Noticing a faintly surprised look on her face, as she opened her lips to reply, he realised he'd somehow said the wrong thing, and went on quickly, "Or has your young man been saying particularly nice things to you?"

Mention of Jack temporarily side-tracked Lily, for it gave her the opportunity to break the news that her wedding was not so distant a possibility as she had at first permitted him to suppose. It wasn't really fair, she had decided, to let him go on assuming nothing definite had been arranged, even though she might be able to persuade Jack to allow her to stay on with the firm after her marriage.

"Well, yes, he has," she replied. "And I'm afraid it's bad news for you, Mr Pelham. That's to say, I'm vain enough to feel you'll think it's bad. Jack and I are getting married in about two months."

"Oh dear!" said Pelham, taken aback. "Meaning you'll want to leave then?" Lily nodded. "That *is* bad news—though splendid from your point of view, of course."

"I'm so sorry about it."

"Nonsense. You mustn't feel like that. At heart every young woman wants to get married, or ought to. And," he added with a twinkle, "it's a

91

bigger career than any job with an unambitious employer and a firm which isn't at all go-ahead, as you pointed out the other day."

"That was the other day," she said gaily, glad she had told him at last. "Things are looking up marvellously now. It's what makes me even more sorry to leave."

"Looking up marvellously," Pelham repeated a little puzzled. "Oh well, I'm glad you think so."

"I certainly do. And now I expect you want all those letters and things. I'll bring them in in a minute. They're nearly finished."

"Ah yes, Miss Clement, thank you," returned Pelham, even more puzzled. He couldn't for the life of him think what letters she was referring to.

Lily retired with a little pout. Why, she asked herself, should he suddenly go back to the "Miss Clement" when three days ago he'd apparently decided to call her "Lily" in future? Perhaps he'd reverted purposely because in spite of apparently taking it so nicely he was annoyed with her for leaving.

But she hadn't had time to shut the door after her before Pelham, who had picked up a typed sheet of foolscap lying on the desk, called her back.

"One minute, Miss Clement, please! What on earth's this?"

Again the "Miss Clement". It seemed to her deliberate. "Am I in disgrace for wanting to go and get married?" she plunged as she came back to his side.

"Eh? What's that?" He forgot the paper for the moment. "No, of course not. What's put that into your head?"

"You're suddenly being so formal," she replied, frankly.

"Formal?"

"Yes. You've been calling me by my Christian name, and now you're..."

Pelham was at once apologetic. The "Lily" must have slipped out once or twice without his realising it. "Had I? I'm so sorry."

"Oh, but I like it. I mean, it's more friendly, isn't it? And I've been with you quite a time, you know."

Pelham considered this statement. Practically all his business friends called their secretaries by their first names: it was just that he personally had always had a slight prejudice against it. He didn't want the rest of his staff to get the idea he was on terms of undue familiarity with any one of them and possibly favouring her at their expense. Silly, now he came to think of it.

"In that case, Lily," he said with a smile, "I shall do so with pleasure. But now"—the smile suddenly faded—"what *is* this document?"

She glanced at it, looked surprised. "Why, that's the résumé of the scheme you worked out with M. Thiers."

"M. Thiers?" Pelham had never to his knowledge heard the name.

"That Paris firm," she explained a little impatiently. "The Frenchman you met for lunch on Saturday."

Pelham sat in stunned silence, realising sickeningly that the double had been at work again. For on Saturday he had lunched at home before going out to meet Travers at Oxmoor.

"Ah, yes, yes of course," he managed at last to murmur.

He laid the paper with excessive care on the desk and stared blankly at it. What on earth had happened? It was impossible that the double had actually been in his office and met this Frenchman.

The girl herself unwittingly supplied the answer. "It *was* a bit of luck, wasn't it, your happening to ring up just at the very moment M. Thiers was here?"

So that was it. The double had telephoned—probably to find out if Pelham was coming in that particular Saturday—had been told by Lily about M. Thiers, and had promptly fixed to meet him for lunch. It was outrageous, and what the precise object was of this new and extraordinary move he couldn't imagine.

He looked at the paper again, Lily waiting at his side. "Memorandum for *Berthier et Cie*", it was headed in Lily's neat typing. A thought struck him. It was obvious the unknown could not have dictated it to the girl, so it must have been written out, after the lunch on Saturday no doubt, and then dropped in the office letterbox. And if so, what about the handwriting: he surely couldn't have imitated Pelham's sufficiently well to deceive his secretary. Or perhaps that had been his reason for entering the flat, to get specimens; and then he had spent the week's lull in practising hard. But even so…

"I'd like to see my original draft for a moment," he said abruptly.

"Do you mean my shorthand notes? It's all I've got. You dictated it yesterday morning, if you remember."

"Dictated it yesterday morning?" repeated Pelham owlishly, not fully grasping what she had said.

"I don't wonder at your forgetting. After all we had the busiest day we've had for——"

Pelham never took in the rest of the sentence. The horrible truth had reached his brain. The double *had* actually come to his office; and had been there all day, while he was away at Crewe. And, worst of all, Lily Clement had never suspected. He now understood her puzzled look when earlier he had remarked that his absence seemed to have done her good. As far as she knew he'd been there on Monday as usual. In a daze he heard her saying:

"Are you feeling quite well, Mr Pelham? You look suddenly white."

With a great effort he pulled himself together. "A touch of——well, it's the heat, I expect."

Though mid-June, the day was not excessively hot and Lily said a little severely: "*I* think it's working too hard yesterday, only you won't admit it. I've never known you *go at* things like that," she added candidly. "Poor Mr Danvers nearly had a breakdown. We cleared up simply masses——"

"I——I hope I didn't drive you too hard?" probed Pelham, a little nearer normal, anxious now to try and find out something more about the double's activities and what he was really after.

"Well, yes. But you made up for it by taking me out for that drink afterwards."

Pelham sat silent again, his brain in a whirl. The unknown had taken her out for a drink——a thing Pelham had never yet done. And, of course, calling her "Lily" must have been his idea too. Why, it looked as though the fellow were out to teach him how he ought to behave. He suddenly laughed, so strangely that Lily looked at him in surprise.

Obviously misinterpreting it, she said: "But I thought it was a charming idea. And we had such an interesting talk too." What on earth had been said, Pelham wondered. "I did enjoy it," she said with warmth, then quickly continued on a lighter note: "After all, settling up that Manson business called for a little celebration, didn't it?"

Manson business?" Once more he found himself stupidly repeating her words, and once more had to make a great effort to pull himself together. "I—I knew they'd written back about that clause, explaining…" He bit off his words: he mustn't let Lily know it hadn't been him. He looked sharply at her, but she had not taken in the implication of what he had said. He caught sight of the file lying in a tray and picked it up.

"I think it's brilliant," Lily was saying. "You've gone right beyond my idea—you know you once asked me what I would suggest. I'm sorry I've been hustling you about it; I didn't know how carefully you must have been thinking it all out."

But Pelham had opened the folder and with the feelings of a child watching a mystifying conjuring trick, was reading the long letter he was supposed to have written yesterday.

It was indeed clever. It accepted their proposals which he'd been chary of doing for so long, but it went further with another suggestion which rather horrified him. He could never send such a… But this was a carbon, the office copy: the letter itself had already gone.

"But I never… I mean, they—they won't agree," he got out desperately. "Not to this."

"You seemed fairly certain at the time. Mind you, I did think it a bit"— she hesitated momentarily for a word—"well, on the crafty side, if you know what I mean. But, as you said, all's fair in love and business," she went on as if quoting. "And you made me see I was being perhaps a little too scrupulous, and that it was all right really."

All *right*, thought Pelham. It certainly wasn't. It was practically dishonest. He'd have to write and call it off. What the devil was the unknown trying to do, he thought miserably. Lily's earlier words suddenly came back to him—"We cleared up simply masses." He realised he had a lot more to find out.

"Will you bring me the copies of—of what we did yesterday? As you said, we did go at it a little, and I just can't seem to get things straight in my head."

"I'll have them in a few minutes. You said, you know, that as it was so late, I could finish the rest off in the morning, and you'd sign them today."

She left the room. Pelham dropped his head in his hands and sat still for some while. Then he pulled the Berthier Memorandum to him and started to read.

At the end of ten minutes he jumped up and paced his office angrily. It was as bad as the Manson letter. The unknown's effrontery was beyond belief. For evidently, he and this M. Thiers had discussed a proposed business association between their respective firms which Mr Pelham of Pelham Lake would never have considered for a moment; discussed it moreover and evidently come to an understanding. And he would have to go back on it. It was an iniquitous position to have been put in, but he could not do otherwise. He'd have to say he'd reconsidered it over the weekend or something: he couldn't tell the Frenchman he'd been talking business with an impostor, knowing by bitter experience that everyone the double had so far met firmly believed he was J. M. Pelham and no one else.

Besides—and here his anger gave place to bewilderment—the scheme was definitely advantageous to him, and he could not make out what the unknown hoped to get out of it himself. Initiating this horrible campaign of spying, impersonation and inexcusable intrusion into his life was understandable only on Travers's assumption that he had some ingenious masterstroke in mind by which he would profit greatly, and presumably Pelham would lose. Yet this scheme and the Manson proposals were undoubtedly profitable to Pelham—if he had been less conscientious in business dealings.

Lily came in with a pile of letters, placed them on his desk and went out. Pelham began to read.

After three-quarters of an hour he was feeling more perplexed than he had ever been in his life—and not a little frightened. The thing was almost uncanny. For the stranger seemed to have delved into every file in the office, and he hadn't the remotest idea *why*. Had his object been merely to acquire a thorough working knowledge of Pelham Lake's affairs—in preparation for whatever coup it was that Travers insisted he was planning—he could just have understood it. But he had gone further. He had carried on the business for him, answered correspondence, made decisions, written letters Pelham himself had been intending to write. More, he had reopened certain matters that had been in abeyance, had made fresh approaches to contacts that had drifted away. No wonder, he thought bitterly, Lily had said in her innocence, "I've never known you *go at* things like that." It was not Pelham who had gone at them. He wouldn't have considered half of it necessary.

Perhaps, he reflected further, he'd been wrong. Lily had always been urging him to be more go-ahead, and this—this combination of an Augean cleansing and a spring offensive was evidently what she had in mind. He recalled her high spirits that morning, her enthusiastic "Things are looking up marvellously". Certainly, she was delighted at what to her was her employer's turning over a new leaf. Already he knew that in her view he was too much inclined to drift along unenterprisingly. Once more he wondered whether the double, as in the case of taking Lily out for a drink and calling her by her Christian name, had been showing him for one day how he ought to run his business. But that was a preposterous way of doing it— insolent, illegal, quite incredible. If only he could lay hands on the fellow, he suddenly fumed, get him put behind bars where he belonged...

And the letters themselves—they were efficient, business-like, and at least one of them very farsighted. He picked it up again. "Gentlemen, While agreeing with your proposal in the main, I envisage certain circumstances which..." Pelham had not envisaged them, but he saw them clearly now. The scoundrel must be devilishly smart to have got such a grip on the firm's affairs in just one day. Nor did they betray his personality in any way: they were to all intents and purposes written by Pelham himself. Not only were the turns of phrase his—though conceivably Lily, who knew him so well, could have been responsible for that—but the lines of reasoning were Pelham's. And yet... He suddenly pushed the pile away from him and, elbows on desk, again sank his head on his hands. He had never written those letters. But— they *were* his letters.

At last he sat up and reached for his pen. He would have to sign them. There was nothing else he could do. He felt inconsequently he ought almost to be grateful. But he wasn't.

As he finished Lily came in. "One more I forgot," she said, giving it to him. Pelham took it almost with foreboding, though he felt nothing more could surprise him. But it was only a covering letter paying an account due to a firm of shippers, and obviously written by Lily as a matter of office routine.

"What about the cheque?" he asked her.

"I have it outside."

"Bring it along and I'll sign it too."

"But it's signed. You did it yesterday afternoon."

Pelham sat up as if galvanised. At last, he thought triumphantly. He'd got him at last. Clever old Ed Travers! One of his suggestions at any rate had proved to be a good one. Trying to control his voice he said as casually as he could, "I'd just like to see it all the same."

He grabbed at the cheque when she brought it. Then the room seemed to spin round him. It was signed with his new signature, the one nobody except his bank yet knew anything about…

12

For the second time that morning Lily was asking anxiously, "Are you quite all right?"

"Y-yes thanks. Just leave me a moment."

She went out looking worried. After a moment Pelham squared his shoulders and called up his bank. From Carter he ascertained that his letter had been received yesterday morning. "I've told my cashiers," he went on, "and we're all set to detect funny business—if that's what you're afraid of."

"And nobody else knows?"

"Of course not. How could they?"

"I mean"—Pelham cast about for just what he did mean—"nobody could have come in with a cheque drawn yesterday, say, but with the old signature, and perhaps learned from the cashier that..." His voice trailed away: he had already realised the absurdity of his query.

"My dear old boy!" There was however a sharp edge to the friendly words. "Aren't you aware that banking's a highly confidential business. Any one of my staff who discussed a client's affairs even on the premises, and even with a close friend of the client's..."

"Yes, yes, of course. Sorry!"

Carter spoke more kindly. "Why don't you tell me what all this is about? You sound worried to death. Besides, I think we've a right to know. After all, *we* may have to stand the racket."

"I'll tell you sometime," said Pelham hastily. "Not now. Sorry to have bothered you."

He replaced the receiver, slumping again in his chair. "Worried to death" was, he felt, an understatement. No one could possibly have known just how to sign that cheque, short of mindreading... He sat up for a moment—perhaps it *was* something like that—then shook his head. Yet there at the foot of the pink slip was his own precisely formed

99

signature, "James M. Pelham"—with the new capital "P"— written by somebody else.

"But *I* am James M. Pelham," he muttered fiercely. "Of Pelham Lake and Co. Jim Pelham! Am I going mad?"

With a sudden shiver he got up and began to pace round the room, trying hard to consider the matter dispassionately. Lily had said the cheque hadn't been signed till the afternoon. Therefore it was just possible that the double had foreseen some such precaution, had gone round to the bank during the lunch-hour on some pretext or other and had found out about it. Carter had pointed out with justifiable asperity that the bank would not discuss a client's affairs even with a close friend, but if it was the supposed client himself…

He went back to the desk and reached again for the telephone to check with Carter, then desisted. He had no idea how to phrase that particular query and would probably only end by offending the other even further. He let his hand drop and sat there staring dully into space.

In her little office too Lily was not working. She was really quite upset about her employer. He was ill; she was sure of it. He'd behaved in a strange manner practically ever since he'd arrived that morning—well, now she came to think of it, ever since she'd told him she was going to leave. Could that have anything to do with it? Perhaps—madly stupid though the very idea was—he had liked her considerably much more than she had guessed, and… But no, though flattering, it was too absurd. She shouldn't listen so much to Joyce's chatter.

On the other hand there *had* been yesterday. She recalled it with considerable pleasure. He'd been absolutely charming all day—and in quite a different manner, one which she'd never suspected. And then the evening—the cocktails and the intimate little talk. She could just imagine what Joyce, dominated by her one idea, would have said had she been present: "Didn't I tell you, Lil, someday he'll start making passes." He hadn't, of course; but there had been a definite suspicion of the possibility, and it had rather intrigued her. She wished he'd shown a bit of that side of himself earlier in their association: life would have been much more amusing.

But of all things he had chosen to reveal this new Mr Pelham on the very day that she'd arranged for Tom to meet him before lunch and see for himself how harmless he was. She giggled out loud at the recollection. It had come out all right in the end, but she'd been a little nervous at first. For having told Tom in all sincerity he was not at all the kind of employer who thought their secretaries fair game, Mr Pelham, she was forced to admit, hadn't behaved like that at all.

Tom had glowered a bit at lunch afterwards and had accused her of deceiving him. "You can tell from his eyes he's not as simple as you tried to make out."

"But he's never been like that before," she had protested. "I suppose it's just that he's in particularly high spirits today. It surprised me. Honestly, it did."

"All that putting his hand on your shoulder and saying, 'I don't know what I should do in the office without your charming little sister!' He'd better watch out for her big brother is all I can say."

"But it's the first time he's ever acted like that," repeated Lily truthfully. "That was one of the things I was surprised at." And had rather liked it too, she admitted to herself. "Besides, if he really had the wicked designs on me you seem to think, he wouldn't want to have anything to do with Jack, would he? And yet only this morning he asked particularly if he could meet him sometime."

"Oh, he's all right, I expect," said Tom with a sudden change of front. "No worse than any of the others. You know, really I rather liked him." He had, in fact, been quite taken with Lily's employer, though he felt in his rather heavily protective manner it was up to him to keep a rigorous watch over his sister's virtue. "He's got personality."

"He liked you too," Lily swiftly followed up. "In fact, he whispered to me just as we were leaving, 'Grand chap, that large brother of yours; I aim to see some more of him'."

"Did he?" Tom flushed with simple pleasure. "He's the type I admire. Obviously knows what he wants. Ruthless, I'd say."

Lily, remembering the more usual Mr Pelham she'd known for eight months, burst out laughing. "I'd hardly call him that. He's much too good-natured."

Tom laughed too. "Have it your own way, Lil. Only mind his good nature doesn't extend to suggesting a little trip to Brighton to put colour in your cheeks."

"Oh, I can cope. But I'll be out of harm's way soon, so he'll have to hurry up. Remember, I told you I've never yet been out anywhere with him even for five minutes."

She had not then known that in a few hours' time she'd find herself drinking gin-and-orange with Mr Pelham at the Strand Palace Hotel. Neither, she thought amusedly in retrospect, had Tom.

But that was Mr Pelham of yesterday. Today... She got up abruptly and went into his office. "I just came to see if you were feeling better."

Pelham pulled himself together. "Yes, thanks, Lily."

And in a small way it was true. He had been looking at the forgery again, and while it was still conceivable that a subtly-handled visit to the bank might have put the unknown wise to the changed signature, there was also the remote possibility that it might have been an accident. His alteration of the capital letter had been very slight, slight enough indeed to have been by an extraordinary coincidence just such a slip as the forger might unconsciously have made in imitating the old one. He should have settled on a much more definite change—if, of course, that *had* been what had happened. He had the uncomfortable feeling that he was wilfully trying to delude himself with a theory he knew in his heart was extremely improbable, but what other explanation was there? None that could be accepted by any human reasoning. "Am I going mad?" he thought wildly to himself once more. He put his hand to his head; suddenly realised that Lily was still standing looking at him, and forced a smile. "It was only a little turn," he got out. "I'm better really."

"Oughtn't you to see a doctor?"

"It's an idea," replied Pelham, suddenly sitting up. It was certainly an idea. But not an ordinary doctor. Something was very wrong with his mind, he was beginning to believe. It was impossible that all these unaccountable things could be happening to him exactly as he fancied they were. He must surely be imagining some of it. He was both frightened and comforted by this thought, like a man shown a dangerous way of escape from a prison. "Yes, it is an idea, Lily," he repeated. "In fact, I might go this afternoon."

"Not this morning? Now?"

"No. I've—I've got a few things to do here."

"It's a wonder there's anything left to do," she laughed. "Oh, I quite forgot. You remember you said yesterday you wanted to meet Jack?"

Pelham nodded vaguely. He was almost past caring now what the double had done or said yesterday. The thing was too big for him. He felt completely defeated.

"Well, I had told him to call for me here this evening, but I can put him off if you'd prefer another day. It's awfully kind of you to have suggested it at all."

Pelham collected himself sufficiently to reply mechanically: "But naturally I want to meet the young man who's taking you away from me."

"Oh, please! You know I don't want to leave. I'm"—how could she explain to him how she'd enjoyed the sudden new companionship of the evening before—"I'm looking forward terribly to getting married, of course, but I don't *want* to leave."

"I know you don't. But marriage is a bigger career than..." He checked himself. He'd said that before. Only that morning too, though it seemed to have been weeks ago. Something *was* happening to his mind. "Of course let your young man come this evening," he went on quickly. "Mind you; it's just possible the doctor might want me to go straight home or something, but then I can always meet him another day."

With a last sympathetic look at him, Lily retired. She was very glad he was going to see Jack because she was convinced that during the last few days her fiancé had had something on his mind, some worry which he wouldn't share with her. Only yesterday, when snatching a quick lunch together, she had pressed him to tell her what the trouble was; and he had denied that there was anything. "Or if there is, it'll sort itself out," he had added, confirming her suspicions.

"Something wrong at the office?"

"Oh no," he replied but not quite quickly enough, and then had changed the subject.

Returning later arm-in-arm to their respective offices, she had tried another tactful approach. "Darling! Did Mr Holbrook say how much the rise was to be?"

"The… Oh, the rise?" His voice was a little harsh. "No, he didn't say. Why?"

"What I meant was"—Lily squeezed his arm tight to her body—"supposing it wasn't as much as you expected, you wouldn't let that postpone our getting married, would you?"

Jack obviously forced himself to laugh. "Lily, my sweet, how you do fuss! Of course we're getting married in two months' time, whatever happens."

"Because," she pursued, "you will remember, won't you, I can always go on earning—till you get a bigger rise." To her surprise she found her voice was almost pleading. She was increasingly aware of how much she wanted to stay on with Mr Pelham.

"I've told you, Lil. *I'm* going to provide the money for my wife… I'm sorry, darling, I didn't mean to sound fierce. It's just that…"

"Darling, what *is* worrying you?"

"Nothing."

She had left it at that, but she was hoping now that if it was something to do with business, as it seemed, Jack might possibly confide in Mr Pelham, provided they got on well together. She decided that she would find some way of leaving them alone when they met.

In his office Pelham again picked up the telephone, this time to ring up Ed Travers, but replaced it almost at once. Ed was no use; Ed with all that wonderful advice about varying his movements, changing his signature and so on. It had done no earthly good at all. And as for his talk about a master criminal preparing some big coup, there had been no evidence yet of any attempt by the unknown to profit, even when he had had plenty of opportunity. Rather indeed the reverse. It almost looked now as though his sole object was to drive his victim—yes, victim; that's what he was—right out of his senses. And he might soon succeed. He pressed his hands hard to his temples as if to steady the brain within. A doctor, a mental specialist—he half-shied away from the word—was the only person who could help him now. The real trouble was somewhere in his mind.

He looked up his diary where he had the address of a man to whom a friend of his had once gone after a bad breakdown, then telephoned. His obvious urgency managed to secure him an appointment for four o'clock that afternoon.

13

Pelham sat in the office, apathetically dealing with routine work, till it was time to go to lunch, then went into the first restaurant he came to. After lunch, he taxied to Hyde Park and walked aimlessly about. He could not believe that it was really himself strolling on the grass, looking at the flowers and the happy children at play. "I'm Pelham—J. M. Pelham," he muttered once or twice and stared at his umbrella, the umbrella J. M. Pelham always carried, as if for confirmation.

At five minutes to four he was on the steps of a house in Wimpole Street. He had not yet pressed the bell; instead, he was wondering what he was doing there. Three weeks ago, even a week only, he would have laughed at the thought of his visiting a mental specialist, because some evilly disposed stranger had on a few occasions posed as him. *I* am James M. Pelham, he thought with determination, and only when a workman engaged in road repairs, said half-humorously, half-kindly, " 'Oo said you weren't, guv?" did he realise he'd spoken aloud.

He turned his back and resolutely put his finger on the bell-push. The workman winked at his mate, as if to intimate that the doctor certainly had a promising customer.

Dr Frazier proved calm, efficient and extremely sympathetic, but before a quarter of an hour had passed Pelham could see that he was baffled. Nor had he been able to tell him everything. Once again, the sheer incredibility of it all held him back. To say that a stranger had come to his office and conducted his business, even to signing his cheques in a manner he had believed was known only to himself, without his secretary even suspecting, was quite out of the question, and he concentrated on the other impersonations which were easier for an outsider to understand.

"Tell me, doctor," he asked desperately at one point, "can this all be hallucinations or something? Or loss of memory? That tie, for instance?" For some reason, the question of the tie left on his dressing-table had come to fascinate him: it was the first thing that had seemed inexplicable by any reasonable standards. For with Rogerson's help he had later checked that all his other ties were there. If then that one had been left behind, the double must have gone away without one, for he would hardly have brought a spare collar and tie specially, just to change into so pointlessly. "I mean, I now have an extra tie, as far as I know. Could I have bought it and forgotten I'd done so? Could I have gone to my Club and played billiards without remembering anything about it? Could I have…?"

"You mean, could *you* be your own imagined double, performing actions of which you have no subsequent recollection?"

"Something of the sort. There's such a thing as split personality."

The doctor smiled faintly. "Yes, but it's quite different from your—your trouble. Besides, I understand from you that on several occasions, when people thought it was you they were talking to, you yourself were actually"—he tapped his glasses on the desk-top—"and could be proved to be in quite another place."

That was true enough, thought Pelham miserably. He'd been at Crewe yesterday, having long talks with his aunt's solicitor and the undertakers, and at the same time Lily was taking down shorthand from the double in London. The double existed, solidly, in three dimensions, and he'd known that all along. He'd only been wildly snatching at straws, desperately hoping for some professional explanation of the inexplicable.

"Then how does he know what I'm going to do and when the coast is clear for him? I can only suppose he's able to read somehow what's in my mind. But you said earlier there's no such thing as telepathy."

"No, I said not in this case. Telepathy exists but almost invariably between two persons intimately associated or mentally attuned. Two total strangers could hardly…"

"But he doesn't *seem* to be a total stranger. If he exists," he almost gabbled. "Does he exist?"

"I think we must accept that he does. Your manservant, the people at your Club, have all…"

"But he *can't* exist," he almost shouted, as if now to convince himself against his reason. "It *must* be something in my mind. Something wrong with my brain perhaps," he added in a low voice, though he felt that even to learn he was mentally deranged would be a relief.

"No. I'm quite positive the trouble isn't in your brain—at least not in the way you are thinking. Naturally, your mind is affected by worrying about it, but not in…"

"How the hell can I help worrying about it?" he burst out.

But Dr Frazier paid no attention beyond a sympathetic gesture. "I can give you something to take, a sedative, that will help to calm your nerves. But the crux of the matter is this: that there is undoubtedly a definite living human being who is doing this."

"I know," admitted Pelham at last. Then, thinking of the signature on the cheque, he added desperately: "If he is human."

"He can hardly be anything else," the doctor said lightly. "But I admit he seems superhumanly clever. And as he is alive and kicking, to use the common phrase, he can be caught—and his kicking stopped."

"Go to the police, you're suggesting? Well, I've done that, and…"

"Actually I wasn't suggesting that. Not at present. They're rather too matter-of-fact. And you are in a very overwrought state. Perhaps after a few days' treatment, you…"

"Treatment?"

"Oh, nothing. Rest, the pills I shall prescribe, very little work at your office, if any, perhaps even a short holiday in the country."

"But then he'll go to my flat again, and…"

"Not if you had a new lock fitted. I gathered from you he's managed to get a copy of your present key."

Pelham brushed this aside. "And worse, to my office." Dr Frazier raised his eyebrows at this. "I didn't mention it before because it's quite incredible. But he was there all yesterday, when I was away. Doing my work for me," he concluded bitterly.

This certainly surprised the other, Pelham noticed. "A whole day! And wasn't caught?" he began. "No, no, of course not, or you wouldn't be here. But he will be soon, if he's doing that sort of thing." He sat silent for a few moments; and then, to Pelham's annoyance, ceased to be the doctor and started suggesting, very much as Travers had done, methods of trapping the unknown. "In short," he concluded, after several minutes of this, "try acting more on impulse. Don't tell anyone where you're going or what you're going to do, till you've done it."

By this time Pelham had become intensely irritated. As soon as possible he brought the interview to a close and found himself outside again in an even more depressed frame of mind than when he had come. He considered Dr Frazier had failed him as badly as Travers had.

He stood irresolute and unhappy on the pavement for moment, then suddenly realised there was nothing in the world he wanted at that minute so urgently as a good stiff drink. Whisky at that—to drag him up out of his depression. Sherry belonged to the old days when a drink was something to be savoured and enjoyed in an atmosphere of carefree contentment.

He looked at his watch—and swore softly. Five to five! He'd have to wait for over half an hour.... No, it was all right after all. If he took a taxi down to the City, the pubs there opened at five o'clock.

Ten minutes later he was sitting on a stool in a bar near Ludgate Circus. He was still unreasonably angry with the doctor. All he'd wanted was medical confirmation that his troubles could be due to some sort of mental disorder. All he'd got were pills, a recommendation to take a holiday and a lot of suggestions that a cheap amateur detective might have made. But slowly he came to the conclusion that he wasn't being quite fair. In himself he now recognised that the double could not be explained away as easily as that: his visit to Wimpole Street had been sheer escapism.

He ordered another large whisky and half-way through it realised that not only was his irritation fading but he was even feeling less worried, less frightened. Inhumanly clever though the double appeared to be he couldn't keep it up. Somehow or other, sooner or later, Pelham would catch him, if he gave his whole mind to it and refused to be rattled by what the unknown did in the meantime.

Yes, he thought, swallowing the rest of his drink at a gulp, that was it. War on the double. He banged his hand on the counter so sharply that people near him looked round in surprise, but he paid no attention. He was going to beat the double. The cunning devil might be smart, but he, Pelham, was going to be smarter.

The barmaid was opposite him with a look of inquiry, thinking he had called for another drink. Why not, thought Pelham, then decided suddenly he'd go to the Club and have it there instead. Maybe the doctor had got something after all with his "act on impulse"! The idea had only that instant come into his head and in ten minutes he'd be there. And maybe the unknown would be too...

He woke next morning with a head, a thing he hadn't had for years. He'd definitely drunk too much the night before, he confessed ruefully; sticking to whisky too, to which he was unaccustomed. The double hadn't been at the Savernake but he'd fallen in with a group of friends up in the bar and had only just got back to Clitheroe Court in time for dinner. He couldn't recollect much about the rest of the evening and wondered if Rogerson had noticed. Then he decided he didn't care. It was nothing to do with his manservant if he chose to have an occasional fling.

And he was delighted to discover that, in spite of his "morning-after" depression, his mood of absolute determination to fight and beat his adversary was still with him. True, it had first been begotten by those two large whiskies at Ludgate Circus but it hadn't died out with the drink.

His head soon yielded to aspirin and he felt quite aggressive as he went up the stairs to his office. If the stranger was there, he'd pretty soon wish he wasn't. A great idea here came to him. When he did catch up with the fellow, he wouldn't waste time over words; he'd set about him good and proper. That'd certainly fetch the police along and achieve a real showdown.

It was not long before he discovered why the unknown hadn't been at the Club the previous evening. Apparently, he'd turned up at the office at four-thirty, almost as if he'd known Lily was half expecting Pelham to do just that.

"Jack was awfully pleased to meet you properly at last," she informed him happily. "It really was very good of you."

Pelham, who'd forgotten all about the tentative appointment, managed somehow to take this in his stride. Now that he was inclining to the belief that the double was not after all planning some major financial operation to his detriment, he suddenly found he was able to worry less about what the other was doing for his own mysterious motives. Indeed, the bolder he became, the sooner would he meet his Waterloo. He resolved to play his part and refuse to let himself be put out of countenance by suddenly learning of things he was supposed to have done.

A tactfully probing conversation with Lily brought out the further information that he had apparently chatted a bit with her and Jack and then, while Lily finished off in the office, had borne the highly flattered young man off to have a drink and a talk, inviting them both subsequently out to dinner with him.

Pelham's new-made resolve not to be surprised was considerably shaken by this last, but he managed to keep his emotions to himself, as Lily went on: "Really, it was most awfully kind of you to take so much interest in us. Particularly in Jack," she added warmly.

Indeed, she was really grateful for the whole evening. Her little scheme of finishing work in the office, and so giving them a chance to talk together alone, had obviously borne fruit, but in what way she did not yet know. For Jack had been in much better spirits all through the meal, though once or twice he had lapsed into a thoughtful silence. And he had displayed no trace of jealousy funnily enough, even though Mr Pelham had behaved, well, really very badly indeed. She laughed pleasurably to herself at the recollection. In fact, he had seemed too over-whelmed by her employer's interest in him to have any such feelings. He deferred to him, laughed at his jokes, called him "sir", and in general carried on as though it had been—well, thought Lily, the great Mr Holbrook himself; while Mr Pelham had teased and flattered her and treated her as an equal. With a little shock she realised that it hadn't been at all like an older man giving a dinner to a young engaged couple, but—and the thought was somehow piquant—like Mr Pelham and herself taking out a young man they wanted to be kind to. She wondered suddenly what had actually passed between them earlier over their drink, and what the apparently now dispelled worry had been; for Jack had been very evasive about it.

"What did you and Jack talk about before I joined you?" she asked Pelham point-blank. "He wouldn't say afterwards."

He gulped, then replied with perfect truth, "I don't think I can tell you. You—you must ask him again."

Though still curious, she did not pursue the matter, glad that whatever it was seemed to have been satisfactorily disposed of.

"I'll get it out of him in time," she laughed, and left the room; leaving Pelham to puzzle his head over the double's extraordinary behaviour. What on earth was he up to, he groaned, his old helplessness and apprehension suddenly coming back to him. But he quickly pulled himself together, reflecting that matters couldn't go on at this rate without something happening.

He remembered then that he had to go down to Crewe early next day for his aunt's funeral and wondered whether he should tell Lily this or not. If he did and the double came to the office, what would be the result? He decided after a time it wouldn't help. Lily would be bound to say something like, "I thought you were going to be away," and the double would catch on quickly and say he'd decided not to go after all. But suppose he rang up Bedford Street from Crewe during the day, to prove he, the real Pelham, was down there?

No, that had happened before, when he'd rung his flat. She'd never believe a voice at the end of the wire, when she knew he was in his office. His only hope was to confront the stranger in person. He verified the time of the funeral and sent for an A.B.C. to check the return trains. If he left as soon as possible after the service, he would arrive at Euston at 4.12 p.m. and could easily get to the office before it shut. As for Lily, he'd just tell her that he might or might not be in tomorrow....

His phone went. It was Rogerson.

"I thought I'd better check with you, sir. There is a person here from Thompson's, the builders, saying he has instructions to change the lock on the front door."

"Oh, that's all right." Pelham had quite forgotten to ring Rogerson about it. He had decided to take Dr Frazier's advice and had dropped in to give the order on the way to the office. "I lost my key," he explained, "and thought it a wise thing to do."

"Of course, sir." Rogerson's tone here indicated he thought it extremely silly.

"There'll only be two keys, and the man will leave them with you. So you'll have to let me in tonight." He made a mental note to dispose of the key he was supposed to have lost. He also reminded himself to buy two keychains which both he and Rogerson would wear in future, or at least till this business was settled. "You can tell the chap to get on with it."

"Very good, sir," Rogerson translated. "I will inform the person he may proceed with the work."

Pelham hung up. Deep inside himself he knew he was still worried and a little frightened, but he felt he was getting on top of it. He was fighting back—and sooner or later he must win.

14

H e got back from the funeral at a quarter past four and taxied from Euston to Bedford Street. He mounted the stairs quietly, paused a moment outside the door of his office to shift his grip on his umbrella, then swiftly entered.

But the room was empty.

He swore softly to himself. Pleading an important engagement he had gone straight from the churchyard to the station, lunching on the train, and really had been confident that this time he would catch his enemy out and put an end at last to the whole abominable business. But once again it seemed that the other had been too clever for him and had not come near the place at all. After all, why should he? For all he knew, Pelham would have been working there as usual. On the other hand—and here he realised with faint surprise that he was already accepting the fact that the unknown in his uncanny fashion could so often guess his movements—perhaps he *had* been in and had left early, aided by that same strange luck, intuition, or whatever it was he possessed. That, he felt, was more probable, and so he was not greatly surprised when Lily, appearing at that moment, gave a little start and said: "Why, hullo! I didn't think you'd be coming back again today."

Her next remark, however, came as a distinct shock. "I do hope it wasn't too trying. I think a funeral, whoever it is, always depresses one terribly."

Funeral! He couldn't imagine how in Heaven's name the fellow had found that out. He was certain Rogerson was the only person who'd known where he was going. But perhaps he'd rung the flat on some pretext, and Rogerson had mentioned it. He pulled himself together and replied a little dazedly: "It was an old aunt of mine."

"Oh, I am sorry! I didn't mean to be so off-hand. But you only said casually 'Just a funeral' this morning when you saw me looking at your black tie."

"But…" began Pelham and was silent. His tie! And of course his black suit. Then the other must have been dressed precisely as he was now, or Lily would have commented. How could he have known the exact clothes to wear? And for what earthly reason had he done it—except that he seemed to be obsessed with the idea of behaving exactly as his victim would do? Had he too gone to a relative's funeral? That would be complete lunacy. Only a couple of days ago Pelham had been wondering whether his brain had been going, now he was beginning to think that it was this double of his who was the mental case. On the other hand he might be doing all this by way of showing Pelham that his whole life was an open book. The thing was beyond him. He could not hope to defeat such an adversary. He was suddenly swamped by a sense of complete helplessness. He was up against something absolutely incomprehensible—and apparently undefeatable. Then he pulled himself together. He must not let himself feel like that. No doubt it was only the effect of the funeral. They were depressing affairs, as Lily had said, and all that standing at the graveside, musing on the transitoriness of life, remembering his aunt as she had been when she was his age and he a schoolboy, had made him more despondent than he need be.

Murmuring something about having only just come along in case there was anything, he left the office. A reassuring glance at his watch showed him that the pubs in the City area would just be open, and he took a taxi along to the same one near Ludgate Circus he had visited the day before yesterday. He'd been drinking too much lately, he knew, but it helped him over these periods of depression, made him feel that if he stuck it out, he must win in the end.

In the pub he ran unexpectedly into two acquaintances in convivial mood, who, learning he had been to a funeral, decided by some quirk of muddled thinking that the only thing for him to do was to drink champagne. By the time he found himself in a taxi on his way home he had regained his self-assurance. More than that, he had come to the conclusion that, just as he must not let himself be put out by suddenly learning things he had presumably done in his absence, so it was no use worrying overmuch about *how* the unknown was able to find out his movements or discover what he was wearing. It was vital to concentrate his full energies on defeating him. He had declared war on his cunning and elusive enemy and must devote himself whole-heartedly to his speedy exposure and obliteration. For, as Dr Frazier had convincingly pointed out, the other was but human, and must make a slip sometime in the increasingly bold game he was playing.

Buoyed up by this revived determination, be began to see that Ed Travers's original advice had possibly not been so bad after all; certainly very much the same suggestions had been made quite independently by the doctor. Unable to talk the matter over further with Ed, who he learned was now away on his summer holiday, he redoubled his efforts along the lines the other had first advocated. He went to the Savernake at unexpected times; once he went out, and half an hour later sneaked back, when Gough for once wasn't looking, and dashed straight down to the billiard-room. He left the office as if for the day and then returned on various pretexts. He announced a visit to the pictures and then looked in at Broad's. He took to going out on some days minus his accustomed umbrella but felt somehow almost naked without it. He even bought himself a new suit of a lively pattern. His tailor would have been horrified, not only at the suit itself but at the fact that it was ready-made. But Pelham didn't care: it fitted him well enough, and there were no similar ones in the establishment as far as he could ascertain, which was his main object. The Double—he had now got to thinking of him with a capital "D" so vivid was his unseen existence and personality—would have difficulty in matching that. He found too, hidden in a cupboard, the jaunty pale brown hat and twice returned to the flat at lunchtime, changed into these for him most unusual garments—to Rogerson's utter horror and disgust and went back late to the office, hoping that the Double had been there in the clothes Pelham ordinarily wore.

Still somewhat obsessed by the tie left behind in his flat, which except for the cigarettes at the Club had been the first material link between himself and his persistently unencountered enemy, he finally purchased, with a flash of what he thought was inspiration, a scandalous red-and-green affair in a small shop in Berwick Street. There was probably not another tie like it in existence the man assured him with a grin, which was just what Pelham wanted. Moreover, ties, he felt, were things which could be changed in a moment, say, between club and office. He kept it handy in his pocket, though quite how he was going to make use of it he wasn't yet certain. And he continued to drink a good deal of whisky, because only by doing so could he maintain his mood of constant aggressiveness towards his invisible adversary.

Rogerson, he could see, was deeply perturbed by his behaviour, and Pelham felt that he was testing him very high. But of course he could not confide in him, could not even tell him that it was only for a short while, and then things would surely be back to normal and his master in his old orderly groove once more. At least, he fervently prayed so: matters couldn't continue at this pitch. If he didn't soon lay the Double by the heels, he—well, he didn't know what he'd do. Indeed, only his belief that this simply must inevitably happen was keeping him going.

Yet just as though the Double had realised this new determination to force a meeting, he now no longer made any appearances at the office or at the Savernake Club or other of his victim's haunts. Nor did he attempt anything at the flat, though Pelham considered he had frustrated him there. The only two keys to the new lock were worn on chains by himself and Rogerson, who had been allowed to infer that this was by the advice of the police owing to recent burglaries in the neighbourhood with duplicate keys.

But he was certainly not idle, as Pelham had soon been made aware. He had, as it were, merely removed his activities from the centre of the circle to its circumference, where there was less danger of meeting Pelham in person and he could yet keep in touch with what he was doing. Worse still, he was obviously up to something mysterious on his own.

It was Lily who gave him the first clue to this. He had just signed some letters—almost mechanically as he did everything now, for nothing mattered except to catch his adversary out—when she said: "Oh, by the way, I have a message for you from Jack."

"From Jack?" repeated Pelham, astonished, for he had never met the young man in question. Then he remembered that on the day he had been expected to do so the appointment had been kept by the Double. "What's it about?"

"He says he has something for you. He'll meet you tonight at six at the usual place."

She spoke casually, as though she'd just given him the most natural message in the world. Pelham found himself automatically replying "Thank you", in the same tone, and she went out.

For some while he sat staring in puzzled fashion at the door through which she had gone; then the implication of what she had said reached his brain. He had thought the Double had only met Jack Benton on that one occasion, but obviously he'd seen him again—and more than once, judging from that phrase "the usual place". What they could have in common he had no idea. He gave a wry smile as he realised that this meeting at any rate wouldn't come off. The wrong man had been given the message.

A little later he broke off his work with a fresh and disturbing thought. If the Double had been meeting Jack Benton behind his back, why not Lily too? He thought he had recently detected signs of a more familiar attitude in her than could be accounted for by their office contacts. He knew the unknown had given her a cocktail and on the following night had taken her to dinner, but he might easily have been seeing more of her since. He accepted that employers who were on friendly terms with their secretaries sometimes did take them out, but not he, J. M. Pelham of Pelham Lake. He felt quite horrified at the thought of members of his staff perhaps seeing them entering a bar or a restaurant together, or otherwise behaving as he would never have dreamed of doing.

Then he cheered up a trifle. Lily was not only a sensible girl, but engaged and in love, and it could easily be that the Double was interested in the pair, perhaps even helping them in his own peculiar fashion—much as he had done that day he had worked so busily at the office, though it hadn't been at all the sort of help Pelham wanted.

This surmise was in part confirmed the next morning. Barely had he arrived when Lily came swiftly in from her room with shining eyes. "I don't know how to thank you," she began excitedly. "Jack's just phoned me about it."

Pelham found himself modestly murmuring, "It's nothing." He'd suffered enough at the hands of the Double: at least he was entitled to some credit for whatever kindness the other had done in his name.

"But it *is*. It's too generous of you. To give him all that money." And before he could say more, she had stepped forward and given him an impulsive little kiss, driving all thoughts out of his head.

He stood staring at her, staggered to observe that she did not seem to appreciate how extraordinary her action had been.

"Sorry, I just couldn't help it," she murmured; and all at once was her own quiet self once more, putting papers in his tray.

Pelham had little idea what was discussed during the next ten minutes while she was in the room. Only when she had gone, was he able to collect himself. He sat for a moment thinking hard. Then he dived into the drawer for the firm's chequebook. The Double, it seemed, had given money, a lot of money, to Jack Benton. Why, he could not conceive, though that was not the immediate point.

But the counterfoils showed that no cheque had been drawn which he did not know about except that first mysterious one to the East End firm which was due to them anyway. His private chequebook he carried on his person, but he examined that to make sure. The safe—but there was never much money in the safe anyway. What *was* going on behind his back?

Yet a further indication of his enemy's mysterious activities came that same morning. He had just left the office to go to lunch when he saw a burly fair-haired young man whose face seemed vaguely familiar crossing to meet him from the other side of the street. For a moment he couldn't place him, then he recognised him as Lily's brother Tom.

But though to his knowledge he'd only seen him once before, and then not to speak to, the young man came up and, almost as if resuming a broken-off conversation, said:

"I was waiting to catch you, sir, as you went out. I've thought over your kind suggestion, and I've decided I'd like to take the job."

Pelham made a non-committal noise.

"It's awfully good of you to offer it to me. I think I see what it entails and"—he suddenly grinned"—it seems right up my street."

Could he say, thought Pelham, that he hadn't the vaguest idea what the other was talking about? No, because the Double knew, and this young man had no suspicion he wasn't the Double.

"I—I'm so glad," he found himself replying helplessly.

"And I understand you won't be ready for me to start till a fortnight. So I'll have time to give my notice in to my employer, and of course I'll have to explain to Lily. Unless you'd wish to?"

This was easy for Pelham. "No—no, you do it," he got out.

Tom looked a little doubtful. "She may not like the idea: you know her feelings about my—about me. But I'm sure you'll be able to put things right if she cuts up rough."

"Yes, yes," muttered the harassed Pelham who felt like shouting: "Go *away*. Leave me alone!"

"Then I'll contact you in a fortnight, sir. And I really am most awfully grateful." He grinned again, this time rather complacently. "*I'll* look after you all right, sir."

And he was gone, leaving Pelham standing dazedly on the pavement. He did not see what he could do. If he told Lily's brother he hadn't offered him a job, he'd look the worst kind of liar. He supposed he'd better wait till he started work and then sack him. It came to him he didn't know even what the job was. The Double was behaving more and more like some sort of evil beetle boring into timber, eating inexorably through all those props and struts which upheld his simple orderly life. Apprehensively he sensed that all this business mysteriously going on between the Double and Lily and her brother and Jack Benton was leading up to something important. And that one day the props might all collapse and his life fall in ruins.

As if he hadn't enough worries of his own, two days later he came back to the office from lunch to find that something had evidently upset Lily while she'd been out. She was a bit red-eyed and inclined to be silent, and Pelham, in spite of his own miserable preoccupations, felt concerned about it. He wondered whether he, or rather that infernal Double, was the cause, but was soon reassured by the fact that whenever he spoke to the girl, she brightened a little and smiled. Rather indeed did she give the impression that he was her one friend in an otherwise cheerless world.

He hesitated, however, to ask her what the matter was, sensing that she was going to tell him but wanted to get the office work out of the way first. He was right. But they were exceptionally busy—thanks to that day a fortnight before, when the Double had visited the office and worked with such unwonted, unwanted, energy—and it was not till nearly five-thirty that Lily came into his office in a resolute manner and stood in front of his desk.

"I had lunch with Jack, and I've found out about the money," she announced in a low voice.

Money. What money, thought Pelham, and suddenly remembered. She must mean the money the Double had so mysteriously given Jack Benton.

"Oh, oh, the money of course," he said vaguely.

Lily was tugging at her finger. Then abruptly she laid her engagement ring on his desk. "You must have it."

"Me? Your ring? But what on earth have I…"

"It was your money paid for it. At least ultimately. So it's yours."

"But why mine——?"

She did not answer him directly, but rushed on somewhat incoherently: "It was so—so *silly* of him. It was only a game choosing it and I never for a moment really thought—though afterwards I had a faint suspicion. But it was practically all his savings. I didn't *really* want that one"—her eye fell on it winking greenly on the blotter—"at least, I did, but not in that way…. All that money! It was our happiness, our security…."

By now Pelham had gathered a rough idea of what she was talking about. Her engagement ring, which he had thought at the time must have been an extremely costly one, had been bought with young Benton's savings and he—or rather the Double—had found out and made him a present of the money. It showed at least that in spite of the cruel way he was treating Pelham, he could be generous. Or was he being generous? He didn't truthfully seem to have that quality in him. It might not have been his own money, or he might even be doing it for some entirely selfish ulterior motive.

With a wry little smile Pelham suddenly realised that he too could be generous—and at no cost to himself. He picked up the ring and held it out.

"*I* don't want it, Lily."

"But I can't take it. It was absolutely *sweet* of you to give him, us, that money"—her voice suddenly held, to Pelham's embarrassment, an almost adoring gratitude—"but don't you see, it's like *you* giving me my engagement ring, not Jack."

"Well, yes. But don't look at it in that way. It is *your* engagement ring and you must keep it and wear it, otherwise your Jack will…"

"I'm not sure," said the girl very slowly and deliberately, "that I want to wear it anymore."

"Oh, but…" The meaning behind her words suddenly struck Pelham and he got up and came round the desk and patted her arm kindly. "Now this is silly," he was beginning, when with a little moan Lily turned and flung herself against him, head on his chest, sobbing quietly.

Pelham was flabbergasted. What on earth had the Double been up to that such familiarity seemed natural to the girl? Then he remembered that she was overwrought, unhappy, and that it was probably only the natural instinct of a child in trouble. Embarrassed, he stroked her shoulder soothingly, and hoped to Heaven Danvers wouldn't choose that moment to come in.

The same thought evidently occurred to Lily for she all at once checked her sobs and drew away. "I'm sorry. I forgot about our being in the office. But you're so—so…" She suddenly blushed through her tearstains and turned away.

"Look here!" said Pelham gently. "It's nearly time for you to leave; I think you'd better go straight away and have a drink or some coffee or something. That'll help pull you together and you'll be able to go home feeling more happy."

"All right," Lily said obediently and went to her room, to reappear a few minutes later freshly made-up and looking as though she'd never shed a tear in all her life.

"Will you come with me?" she asked. "Join me soon, of course, I mean. The Tivoli bar, you know."

"I—I—" He didn't know how to answer this amazing suggestion. Gratefully he saw the ring on the desk and used it as an excuse not to reply. "Here! Don't forget this!" he said quickly and gave it to her.

About to put it in her bag, Lily looked at him, and then with a funny submissive little smile drew it on to her finger. "I suppose that's best after all, isn't it?" she said and went.

Pelham slumped abruptly in his chair in complete bewilderment. Most certainly something was going on and he wished to Heaven he knew what it was. Lily's behaviour—apart from the outburst—had seemed to indicate that she and the Double were on very friendly terms. Why, she'd actually asked him to go out with her. And the Tivoli bar round the corner in the Strand was mentioned as though they had been there before. He only hoped none of his staff visited the place when they... He choked with sudden anger.

That infernal blasted Double! He slammed his fist with silent force into his palm. But he'd get him yet—and stop all this before it had gone too far.

15

"It really *was* sweet of you to talk to me like that," said Lily suddenly about halfway through the next morning. "What you said was so—comforting and sensible."

She spoke with such obvious depth of feeling that Pelham was puzzled. He could not believe that he had said anything much more than would be normal in soothing a young woman in an emotional crisis and made some remark to that effect.

"Oh, I don't mean that," she replied. "I mean in the evening—in the Tivoli."

Pelham swore to himself. He had missed the Double again, largely by his own stupidity. Last night in his newly recovered mood of angry determination he had gone hopefully first to Broad's and then to the Savernake: if only he had fully taken in from what Lily had said that the Tivoli was a meeting-place for them, he might have caught him out at last. But would he? he thought further. Somehow, his unknown enemy never *was* anywhere when Pelham went there too. And if not, and he himself had gone, Lily would naturally have assumed that he had come to join her after all, just as though he were—well, chasing her like some employers did. What impossible positions his enemy was putting him in!

"I do see what you meant about Jack," Lily was continuing. "I'm having lunch with him today, and I'm really going to have it out, as you advised."

And here, thought Pelham bitterly, was yet another impossible situation. He had no idea what to say, for he didn't know what she was talking about—except that it was probably about the ring, and that things seemed to be going badly between the young couple. "But, Lily," he ventured, trying to put matters right if he could, "you should remember that buying an expensive ring for the girl one loves may be silly, but at least it shows…"

124

"It's not that only," she cut in decisively. "There's all the other things we talked about. You've opened my eyes, you know."

Pelham, though still at sea, didn't like the sound of this at all, and tried again. "You mustn't do anything rash. After all, you love Jack and he…"

Again she interrupted. "That's not what you…" She broke off. "You are somehow so different at times. I suppose it's this being in the office. You did tell me about that, didn't you—secretary and employer—and here I am breaking our rule." She came round the desk to stand by his chair, and her voice suddenly became warm and affectionate. "I do rely on you so," she half whispered. But before the astounded Pelham could make any reply, she was all at once her normal self, saying matter-of-factly, "It's Tuesday. Don't forget you have that appointment at two-thirty with Warners in Aldgate."

"N-no, I remember," stammered Pelham, his mind still puzzling over this strange new side of Lily that had been revealed during the last few days.

"I expect you'll go straight there from lunch, won't you?" She laid a sheaf of papers in front of him. "And you'll need to study these before the meeting. It's important, you know." She laughed. "May mean a lot of money."

"Of course, yes." Pelham essayed to look interested. What the hell did money mean to him in all his personal troubles? He could think only of the way his ordinary normal life was slowly being completely destroyed.

He didn't get back from Aldgate till about five o'clock, tired and dispirited. The long meeting had not gone well: his thoughts were elsewhere all the time. With a certain grim humour he found himself reflecting that if only the Double had been there instead it would no doubt have been highly successful from the firm's point of view.

No sooner was he seated at his desk than Lily came in carrying a file.

"Well, I've done it," she announced as she walked across the room. Her voice seemed strangely, almost purposely, devoid of expression.

"Done what?"

"What you said I might have to do." She was still matter-of-fact, though evidently holding herself in. Very carefully she laid the file in his tray and then, just as Pelham had noticed with sudden concern that she was no longer wearing her engagement ring, she burst out in a low intense voice: "It was the last straw. On top of that idiocy about the ring he actually suggested that we put the wedding off because Mr Holbrook had changed his mind about the rise, or hadn't really meant this coming summer, or something silly—I just wouldn't listen to all of it. I don't believe his precious Mr Holbrook ever really said anything about a rise at all." The words came tumbling out faster, though she at once checked her mounting tones as Pelham glanced apprehensively towards the door of the main office. "Jack probably only made it up to show how important he was. Or just to get me. I was quite happy as I was," she went on defiantly. "The whole thing—the whole thing is absolutely…" She choked on a sob. "Well, it's as you said."

Dumbfounded at her outburst, Pelham tried uneasily to produce something soothing, but the words wouldn't come. Lily had obviously broken off her engagement; equally obviously it seemed the Double had had a good deal to do with this, and he now had suddenly a horrible suspicion that he was going to be blamed for it. "I'm most terribly sorry about all this," he got out at last.

Lily's incipient tears vanished at once. "Oh, it's not *you*," she replied in the same warm affectionate voice she had so unexpectedly used that morning. "You've been the one big help in it all. But for you I'd…" She broke off and stood looking queerly at him. Then her eyes dropped, she turned on her heel, and was gone.

This, thought Pelham to himself, was the last straw. Three emotional scenes with his secretary in two days—and nothing whatever to do with him. He almost felt like screaming out loud at his utter helplessness. Mechanically, he picked up the file she had laid in front of him. His hands gripped it tight in sudden fury. How could he ever work again? He started to tear it across, as at that moment he would have liked to do to the Double—tear him slowly apart till he ceased to exist anymore. Then he flung it angrily into a tray, got up, took his hat and umbrella and was making for the door when Lily reappeared. Pelham braced himself for whatever was yet to come, but she merely asked calmly, "Are you going?"

"Yes," Pelham almost snapped, and she instantly looked concerned. "I'm sorry," she said simply, "I do worry you, don't I? I don't mean to."

She smiled happily across at him. "I want to do anything but that. Will you meet me at the Tivoli again this evening?"

"I shan't be there tonight," said Pelham coldly. He just stopped adding, "And I wasn't there last night either," but decided that would be unkind to the girl, who after all was not to blame for all this.

"Oh please! You must," she pleaded passionately. "I need you. I'll go anyway, in case you change your mind."

She looked so forlorn, so dependent on him, that all he could say was, "Well, I'll see about it," realising that if he didn't go, the Double, in the mysterious way he had of foreseeing his movements, probably would; and as far as the girl was concerned, that would do as well. Better even; for, without knowing it, it was the Double she really wanted to talk to, not him. Besides, this unhappy mess was all the other's doing: let him deal with it.

He was rewarded by a sudden radiantly happy smile and a heartfelt "Oh, *thank* you!" As she went back to her room she said almost wickedly over her shoulder: "You're so much nicer outside the office."

Pelham was left open-mouthed. He just couldn't believe that it was his demure little Miss Clement speaking like that. With a helpless gesture he went out.

In the street he paused, wondering unhappily where to go and what to do. A thought struck him. Here surely was his chance at last, the chance he had missed last night. He would change his mind and go to the Tivoli after all; a little later on, say. By then almost certainly the Double would have taken advantage of his intention not to go... But no, his aggressive mood seemed to have deserted him. He felt empty, despondent, beaten. What had *happened* to his pleasant orderly life? If only the last six weeks could be obliterated and he could be strolling cheerfully along as of old, to drop into Broad's for a sherry, or taking a taxi to the club for billiards, or *en route* to the cinema. All these things were poisoned for him now. Except, he realised with faint surprise, the cinema. He hadn't seen a film for a month. For that very reason no doubt that was the one place where the Double had not impinged upon his normally ordered existence. The mere thought of the dim friendly security of the auditorium, the temporary effacement of all his worries as he was absorbed into the events on the screen, suddenly cheered him up. He bought an evening paper, turned to the Amusement Guide and saw that there was something on at the Odeon which looked as though it might be interesting. He entered a phone box.

"It's me, Rogerson. Mr Pelham," he said. For a moment he held his breath, remembering the call of a fortnight before; then, fingering the keychain that snaked securely into his pocket, realised that that could not happen again. "I'm going to the pictures and shan't be back to dinner."

"Very good, sir." Pelham detected a note of irritation behind the respectful tones. His master's frequent changes of plan were obviously getting on Rogerson's nerves.

"I hope it hasn't upset your arrangements," he went on apologetically. "Would you leave some cold supper out for when I get back?"

"Certainly, sir. At what hour will you return?"

"Let's see. Say about a quarter to ten. But you can go to bed."

The conscientious Rogerson, however, rejected the idea. "I should prefer to wait up, sir."

"All right, then. I may be earlier, if I don't like the picture."

He replaced the receiver and looked at his watch. His spirits rose as he saw that it was five-thirty. He could go and have a drink or so and possibly a sandwich till it was time for his film.

Watching the screen in the cool darkness, Pelham passed the happiest two hours he had had for weeks, for the film was exceptionally good and held his attention every minute. It was with quite a shock that he found himself at last snatched out of its pleasant make-believe world into the harsh reality of his harassed existence.

Letting himself into his flat a little after half past nine he was surprised to find the hall in darkness. He supposed that the normally punctilious Rogerson had for once forgotten to turn on the light. Switching on, he hung up his hat and umbrella and went into the sitting-room, thence through to the dining-room. But instead of the neatly set-out meal he was anticipating, only the bare polished surface of the table winked the light back at him, mirroring the central bowl of roses.

Really, thought Pelham, this was too much. He'd distinctly told Rogerson to leave out some supper, and there could have been no misunderstanding because the other had replied "Certainly, sir", and had asked what time he'd be in. Or possibly—for Rogerson suddenly had new ideas as to how things should be done—he'd taken a tray into the bedroom.

At that point it occurred to him to wonder where exactly Rogerson was. It was his invariable custom to greet his master on his return home, and he'd said he'd wait up. Perhaps he'd been taken ill suddenly; that would account also for the light not being on.

He was about to go to Rogerson's bedroom when the latter appeared. He was in his shirtsleeves, minus collar and tie, evidently halfway to bed. His mouth fell open in surprise as he recognised Pelham, then the normal mask of deference descended on his face as he said: "I'm extremely sorry, sir. I heard someone moving about in the dining-room. I did not realise it was only you."

"Who else should it be?" snapped Pelham. "And what about supper?"

Rogerson's mouth again fell open. "Supper? But you've had some," he replied almost angrily.

"I—I've *what?*"

With an obvious effort the other regained his composure. "You've had your supper, sir." Evidently deciding his master had been drinking and must be humoured, he adopted an indulgent tone. "You had cold chicken and salad, and cheese, and a half bottle of the Liebfraumilch, and—and you seemed all right then." Hastily he corrected himself and went on solicitously, "I mean, I can see you aren't quite well now."

Pelham perceived what was in Rogerson's mind. "Look here! I'm not drunk," he burst out irritably, "if that's what you're hinting."

"Sir!" Rogerson was quite affronted, not, Pelham could see, because he hadn't been thinking that, but because it had been so crudely put into words. "Not on one small bottle of wine, sir." All the same the implication was left that he *had* found his master in the dining-room where the whisky decanter was.

"But I haven't even..." Pelham suddenly stopped short. To him was now coming the only possible explanation. No, surely, impossible, he thought, dropping his hand to the keychain. The Double simply could not have got in, let alone have eaten his supper.

He found he must have said the last words half aloud, for Rogerson, still eyeing him a little dubiously, said in soothing tones: "Why, yes, you did, sir. Surely you…" An idea occurred to him. "One minute, sir."

"I tell you I…" began Pelham wildly, following him out. But the other had gone into the kitchen opposite. He waited in the passage and in a moment Rogerson rejoined him, carrying an empty wine bottle and a garbage pail. "See, sir! The Liebfraumilch bottle!" And then lifting the lid of the pail he pointed out, recently deposited on top, chicken bones, cheese rind, and a few limp remains of a salad.

Pelham stared dazedly at them while Rogerson watched him sympathetically. He realised now that his master had not taken too much to drink, but really was ill in some strange fashion he could not understand.

"Did *you* have any supper?" Pelham asked desperately. "Any chicken, I mean?"

"Oh no, sir. Just a small piece of pork pie. At my usual time, eight-thirty. In fact, I'd only just finished when I heard you return. I hadn't expected you so early, but assumed the film was not up to expectation. And then, as you know, I came in to ask if the Liebfraumilch I had got out was suitable for you, as we had so little of it left."

But, thought Pelham, when he was able to collect himself, all this was terrible. It was not, as on the previous occasion, a case of Rogerson merely glimpsing the Double briefly. He had seen and spoken to him—and had, like everyone else, even Lily, been completely deceived. And—what else was that he had just said, that he had heard him return? His hand went again to his pocket to feel his latch-key; he could see the chain of Rogerson's snaking into a trouser pocket. It was beyond all human power. He felt suddenly sick and put his hand to his stomach.

"Shall I get you a glass of water?" Rogerson, upset, was at his side, but Pelham waved him away. "You are evidently unwell. And you should go back to bed."

"Back to bed?" croaked Pelham. "I haven't been yet."

"I beg pardon. I quite thought you had. About half an hour ago you said good night and went into your room and naturally I…" A faintly puzzled look came into his eyes. "Besides, I then retired myself and as you know one wall of my room adjoins yours. I heard the basin running and later the springs of the bed as you got in and the click of the bedside light going off—everything just as I so often do. In fact, sir, had it been anyone else but you yourself here in the passage now, I'd have told them, 'Mr Pelham's in his room and in bed'."

Pelham stared vacantly at him for a few seconds. Then snapping out "Come with me!" he ran to the hall, down the other little passage to his bedroom and flung open the door, at the same time switching on the light.

The room was empty, but the bed was rumpled, with the covers thrown back; slippers were on the floor, pyjamas tossed in a chair. Pelham's head seemed to spin round and he put his hand on the doorpost to steady himself. Then he darted to the bed and felt it. It was warm. He looked under it, quickly flung open cupboard doors, pushed past Rogerson, still carrying the garbage pail and staring at him in bewilderment, searched the small room opposite and the adjacent bathroom and returned breathing heavily. Noticing at last his manservant's utter consternation he mumbled in lame excuse: "Thought I heard someone in my room!'

Obviously not believing, Rogerson looked at him queerly, but made no comment. Instead he pointed at the tumbled sheets and said: "You see, sir, you have been in bed."

"Are you quite sure you…" He stopped. Still searching wildly for some natural explanation to cling to, he'd been about to ask whether Rogerson had remembered to make the bed that morning but had at once realised the absurdity of such a question. Besides, it had been warm. He knew now without a shadow of doubt it had been recently occupied and not by him.

But Rogerson had not been paying attention. He was dumb-foundedly scratching his head. "But I heard you put your bedside light out. And that was only a few minutes before I next heard you in the dining-room. You *can't* have got up and dressed in the time. What the hell is…" He bit the words off quickly. "I'm sorry, sir." Quick sympathy came into his eyes. "I fear you are not at all well. Should I ring the doctor?"

"No, no. I'm all right. Just a…" He could not collect his thoughts, hardly knew what he was saying. "Must have been a bad dream or something. Yes, that's it. I dreamed a burglar was in the flat," he went on rapidly, words tumbling out. "Only a dream about a burglar. I'll be all right." He walked to the basin and poured himself a glass of water. "Just leave me. Leave me. Good night, Rogerson."

Rogerson paused, hand on the door for a moment, as if doubtful whether he should go, his worried gaze on his master. Then, "Good night, sir," he replied gravely and left.

16

Slowly, Pelham sipped the water. Then he turned, stared round the once familiar room which now appeared strange, even sinister, for barely ten minutes ago it had been occupied by the Double. The Double whom he had been trying so hard to catch without ever getting near him, who had seemed latterly to have removed his activities outward from Pelham himself to Lily and her brother and Jack Benton, had now returned to the attack. And once more he had come to the flat—though neither of the two keys could have been in his possession—eaten supper and gone to bed. It was yet again, as on his first visit, just as Pelham himself would have done.

And now he was no longer there. But according to Rogerson only a few minutes had elapsed between his hearing the bedside light go out and coming out of his room to see his master in the dining-room. The time they had spent in there had been quite brief, for when Rogerson went to the kitchen to fetch the garbage pail Pelham had followed into the passage, whence the hall was in clear view. And there they had both stayed, till the moment when Pelham had rushed into the bedroom. Was it humanly possible that anyone, hearing his key in the lock, could have got up, dressed, stolen across the hall and out of the flat during the short while he had been in the dining-room? He simply could not believe that it was. Even less humanly possible did it seem that he could ever have got in. And if none of this was *humanly* possible...

His knees began to shake and abruptly he sat on the bed. He knew now why quick unreasoning terrible fear had suddenly gripped him on those occasions when he had been confronted with some more than usually inexplicable move by his adversary—the joke about the cannon, the signature on the cheque, the foreknowledge of the funeral. Always he had fought it down, fought for and clung to some explanation however far-fetched; and latterly he had managed to thrust the wild thought to the back of his mind by working up an angry determination to catch the Double out. But it had all been mere whistling in the dark, beating the air. The Double *could* not be caught out. "He's only human, he'll slip up sometime," Dr Frazier had said. But he would not slip up, because—because…

He bowed his head in his hands, his mind a pool of unformed horror. What he was up against could surely not be of this earth. Fearfully, like a schoolboy starting to explore some dark eerie cavern which he does not want to enter but by which he is as much fascinated as repelled, he tried to recall all he had read about ghosts, about spirits who had taken human shape. It was unbelievable, but what then was it? Nothing made any sense to his tortured brain; nothing was real—except the unknown Terror steadily engulfing his life. He broke into an uncontrollable fit of shivering and raising his head looked fearfully round the empty room.

"What do you want of me?" he whispered to the empty air through quivering lips. Then, "Why *me*? What have *I* done bad enough to deserve this?"

With a sudden impulse he rolled sideways off the bed on to his knees and tried to pray. But he had not prayed for so long the words would hardly come, and then not with any real meaning. Though at odd moments, whenever he thought about it, he had considered that by being honest, cheerful, kindly and generous to his neighbour and refusing to think evil of anyone he was managing to live a reasonably Christian life, his religion had drifted away from him many years ago. Perhaps that was why this had happened, he thought miserably, gabbling fragments of half-remembered prayers.

After a long while he struggled up hopelessly from his knees and flung himself face down on the bed, more wretched and more scared than he'd ever been in his life.

How long he lay there he did not know, but twice he dozed off and woke with a sudden start, sweating clammily. On the second occasion he started for the dining-room in search of a drink but stopped halfway. Even that, he knew, would be no good. Trembling now with cold from his sweating and lack of food, he finally forced himself to undress and go properly to bed, even though he shuddered at the memory of the last occupant. But he could not sleep. How could he ever sleep again, he asked himself, with this—this Other somewhere, anywhere, everywhere, inexorably infiltrating into his very existence? No wonder all his moves and plans were known if the Double possessed supernatural powers, if It was—he hardly dared face the thought—itself a creation of the supernatural.

"What can I do? What can I do?" he found himself asking aloud, his brain racing round and round like some trapped animal. There must be something: he felt he'd go mad if there wasn't. Someone must be able to help him—even in a matter like this, even against whatever the Double was. He could not remain alone with his trouble. A clergyman, of course—the answer suddenly occurred to him. But he couldn't go blindly up to just any priest and tell him the fantastic story. It must be someone of common sense and understanding. He tried to recall the various clergymen he had known, and in the midst of this with a little sob he suddenly dropped into exhausted sleep.

But he woke again long before it was time for Rogerson to call him and in the fresh early morning light felt a little less miserable. For with his short sleep, he found, had come the answer to his final overnight question.

Nearly a quarter of a century ago when he was at school there had been a parson on the staff who taught Scripture and English, and incidentally was sports master. He was a cricket Blue and largely because of this the boys, Pelham among them, thought a good deal of him, confided in him, took their troubles to him. Fanbury was his name —"Fanny" he was called, of course—and Pelham had kept in touch for a while after leaving school. And about twenty years ago, he recalled receiving a letter from Fanbury, saying he had been given a living somewhere in Devonshire by the good offices of his uncle who'd been made a Bishop, and hoped that any of his ex-pupils would look him up if they were in the neighbourhood.

Pelham had made a note of the address but wondered whether he would be there after all this time. Still, clergymen often settled down in country parishes for years and years and it'd be a starting-point—if, of course, he suddenly thought with sinking heart, Fanbury was still alive.

Jumping out of bed, for he could not wait to grasp at this last lifeline, he flung on his dressing-gown and went to the desk in the sitting-room. Here he encountered Rogerson dusting.

"Why sir," he said in pleased surprise, "I thought you'd be staying in bed today. You are better, I trust?"

"I think so," said Pelham. It was true the daylight seemed to have dispersed his fears a little, but the horrible thing was still with him though he tried to thrust it into the back of his mind for the time. Fanbury would help him, he felt certain, if anyone could.

"Even so, might I advise a doctor?"

"I'll see later," muttered Pelham, already at the desk and pulling out old address books, methodically stowed away. "I'll have breakfast as soon as it's ready," he said over his shoulder. "I'll bath and dress afterwards."

Shaking his head in worried manner—for never had his master done such a thing—Rogerson left the room.

After a while he discovered what he was looking for. "Fanbury, G. N. (Rev) Ossingford Vicarage, nr. Newton Abbot, Devon." He wondered if he were still there but didn't know how to find out. The matter was too urgent to write, possibly receiving an answer after several days to say he'd left years ago. It was Friday: if Fanbury were still there he could go down today, stay in the neighbourhood over the weekend to thrash the matter out and get the help and guidance he sorely needed. Impulsively he laid his hand on the telephone. It was very early, he knew, but someone would answer who could tell him at least if Fanbury was still Vicar.

He obtained the Vicarage number from "Inquiries" and soon was on tenterhooks listening to the bell forlornly ringing. After a while, a countrywoman's voice answered him, breathless and a little annoyed.

"Is Mr Fanbury still Vicar of Ossingford?" he asked.

"Yes. And has been these twenty years." Pelham gave a sigh of relief. "But he's still in bed. If you ring again after nine, he'll be up."

"Thank you. Would you tell him Mr J. M. Pelham rang, and will phone again just after nine. He may not remember me, but say I was a boy at Kenton School when he was a master there."

The woman assented curtly and put the receiver down. So that was all right, thought Pelham, feeling a little happier. He got out the A.B.C. and looked up trains. He'd take the very first one available after he'd rung up, and let the office go hang. He found one at ten-thirty and, Rogerson bringing in breakfast at that moment, he told him to pack a bag for the weekend and order a taxi for ten o'clock.

He ate his breakfast like a man in a dream, turning over in his mind the previous evening's events: wondering whether after all they could really have happened exactly as he thought they had. Wasn't it just possible that the Double had got out of the flat quite normally? If he had heard the front door, he would have had all the time that Pelham was hanging up his hat, going to the dining-room, finding no supper, being discovered by Rogerson, and talking with him, right up to the moment when he followed him out into the passage. It must have been longer than he thought. On the other hand, he could not understand why the Double had come to the flat at all and actually gone to bed, when he must have known Pelham would be coming back, and might even have gone straight to the bedroom—*unless* he had perfect confidence in his own supernatural power. Supernatural power! He found himself whispering the horrible words aloud. For, apart from any of his subsequent actions, even if they could be explained, he had entered the flat normally—with a key; Rogerson had heard him. And there were only two keys, both of which... His overnight terror flooded back on him. He simply must see Fanbury as soon as possible.

He gulped down the last of his breakfast, had his bath, dressed quickly and came back to the sitting-room again to find it was still only a quarter to nine. He sat down impatiently by the telephone, assailed now by the fear that something might yet go wrong, that for some reason Fanbury wouldn't be able to see him. Again he tried hard to convince himself that the Double was just an ordinary human being, cruel and malevolent though he was, who had somehow managed to get into the flat, have supper, go to bed; and then, being disturbed, get swiftly out again unseen—anything to force the horrible unbelievable alternative out of his mind.

While waiting it occurred to him that he ought to tell Lily he wouldn't be in that day. It was early, he knew, and she probably wouldn't have arrived, but one of the junior clerks would certainly be in and take the message.

But it was Lily herself who answered, all at once gay and lively when she learned who it was.

"You sound very happy," he said dully, faintly surprised that anyone could be when the whole world seemed to him steeped in gloom. "You weren't when I last saw you."

"Oh, but I *was*. You know I was really. It was just that I wanted time to think about things."

Pelham took a moment to realise that of course she must have met the Double after all last night at the Tivoli and was referring to that. His stomach contracted sickeningly. The very thought of it now sounded horrible, obscene. "You were a darling to meet me after all. And the lovely dinner. I don't often have champagne. It makes me quite—quite reckless, don't you think?"

"Does it?" he stammered.

"You should know," she replied, her voice warm and vibrant, yet now with a queer undercurrent of feverish excitement which somehow stirred and at the same time frightened him. He'd never heard her speak like that before. "Well?" she went on in low eager tones.

"Well what?" he got out.

"Aren't you going to ask me what I..." She broke off, and Pelham guessed that one of the clerks must have come into the room. In a swift, excited little whisper she said, "The answer's yes," and rang off.

Pelham stared confusedly at the receiver for a moment before replacing it. Then he made a move to pick it up again. He'd never told her that he wouldn't be in that day: the extraordinary conversation had driven it right out of his head. But as he lifted it and the instrument burred inquiringly at him, he changed his mind. What was the use of telling her he was not coming when for all he knew his place might be, probably would be, taken by that other, that evil... He couldn't form the word. He simply *must* have guidance, comfort, and help.

He looked again at his watch. It was almost nine at last.

By a quarter past the hour it had all been fixed—though not as happily as he could have wished. Fanbury had been obviously delighted to hear from him, but when Pelham said he'd be spending the weekend just a few miles away at Newton Abbot and would like to look him up, there'd been no suggestion of an invitation to the Vicarage instead, as he'd secretly hoped. What he had to say could be so much more easily put in one of those long chats over a drink before going to bed. Indeed, to Pelham's disappointment, the clergyman had even excused himself from asking him over that day, as he had several committees and also his sermon to prepare, but fixed a meeting for Saturday morning at eleven. Pelham had of course to fall in with this, but comforted himself with reflecting that once the other had grasped the magnitude and importance of his problem, there was still most of the weekend for further talk.

As he put down the receiver, he realised that there was now no need for him to catch that ten-thirty train if he was not seeing Fanbury till Saturday. He could even go down to the office after all and if the Double were by chance there… But no. He shivered suddenly at the idea. He was desperately afraid of that meeting now. At least till he had seen Fanbury.

17

The Rev Mr Fanbury was cutting roses from a central bed in the smooth-mown front lawn of the Vicarage. He put down basket and scissors as soon as he saw his visitor and hurried to meet him, peeling off his gardening gloves.

"My dear fellow! How charming of you to come and see me!" He shook hands warmly. "Yes," he twinkled, looking him up and down, "in spite of the hand of Time I can still detect young Pelham of the Upper Fifth, and—let's see—slow leg-breaks, wasn't it?"

"That's it. But only Second Eleven."

"Well, never mind… Aren't my roses beautiful? Come round to the summerhouse. I have sherry ready there. I find a mid-morning glass an excellent idea—on special occasions of course. But then this is indeed a special occasion. I haven't seen an Old Kentonian for about two years now, in my remote village fastness. Stubbington Major it was, but I believe he was after your time."

Twenty years, thought Pelham as he followed, had done a lot. The incisive tones and vigorous wording with which "Fanny" had given straightforward advice on juvenile problems or encouraged hesitant batsmen had been blurred down to the smooth intonations and rounded phrases of a typical parson; and he would never have recognised the spare forthright figure he recalled from schooldays in this elderly, benign and rather plump man with white hair, well dug into what was evidently a most comfortable benefice. But, he reassured himself, in whatever fortunate circumstances Fate—with the obvious help of his uncle the Bishop—had placed him, he was still Fanbury, who had been a tower of strength in school-boy days, and he was still a priest of God.

After a few memories had been exchanged, Pelham said tentatively: "As a matter of fact I've looked you up for a rather special reason. I'm in—in great trouble."

Quick and genuine sympathy flowed from the other. "I am so sorry. If there's anything—anything at all—I can do, you may certainly count on me."

"Thank you. You were always so good at advising and helping us as boys, that naturally I…" His voice trailed away. How on earth could he begin?

"What sort of trouble is it?" asked the other gently.

With a little gulp Pelham came straight to the point. "I'm being—well, persecuted—frankly, that's the only word—by someone who's exactly like me in every way—face, voice, clothes…"

"Clothes? One minute! I can understand the accident of physical similarity, but…"

"That's just it. He's made himself like me on purpose. He's pretending to *be* me. And he's slowly encroaching more and more on my life. You can hardly believe how much. He not only meets my friends at my own Club, but he comes to my office in my absence, and he's so like me that not even my secretary knows. In fact, he's interfering in her private affairs and meeting her fiancé as me, and he's offered her brother a job in my name; and, worst of all, he goes to my flat when I…"

He stopped abruptly at the look on the clergyman's face. In his eagerness for help and advice he'd let himself be carried away by the recital of his troubles. He was asking the other to swallow too much at once. He started again and spent a full quarter of an hour explaining how from at first merely thinking he had a double who was either indulging in practical jokes or planning a crime, he had come to realise the unknown was, it seemed, deliberately trying to become a second Pelham. "He's sort of taking over my life—and not as I live it, but as *he* would live it, if you understand what I mean."

Fanbury nodded a little hesitantly "Most extraordinary," he murmured at last, and then again: "*Most* extraordinary!" He knitted his forehead. "But if, as you say, this person's object is apparently not material gain, then…"

Pelham held up his hand. This was the moment he had been leading up to. "One minute! Is it really a *person*?" he asked slowly. "Or something more?"

"I don't quite follow. What more could he be?"

Rather shamefacedly, Pelham said: "One hears sometimes about such things as ghosts, or rather evil spirits, things that aren't—well, human?"

Fanbury looked a little shocked. His reply seemed to Pelham to be automatic, almost platitudinous. "There are evil men in the world, certainly, who seem to us to be of the Evil One himself, but…"

"I'm certain it's *more* than a man," Pelham burst out, "however evil." He was beginning to feel suddenly unhappy. This was not the Fanbury he had come to meet, the Fanbury he'd known when a boy. Or maybe it was, and he had never progressed further than what he had then been, and even that was now swathed tight in twenty comfortable years. He must *make* him understand—and help. "He, it, whatever he is, can't be human. He knows my inmost thoughts, what I'm going to wear, where I'm going, what I'm about to do, even as I decide to do it—and yet is never *there*."

"But surely that's impossible." The older man was obviously distressed on his visitor's behalf. "He *must* be there. You say people, friends of yours, talk to him, are wilfully deceived by…"

"He's never there when I am, I mean. Last night he was the other side of a door, but the room was empty when I went in." He told Fanbury in detail about the Double's visit to the flat.

"But of course the scoundrel must have slipped out when you were in that other room."

"Yes, yes. I thought that, tried to think that, but I realise now he couldn't have done it in the time. And the getting in—just the two keys, on chains. Surely only someone not—not of this earth…"

"He could have copied the key." Pelham made an impatient gesture; then he saw that the other did not really quite believe this last himself, was merely automatically resisting acceptance of anything supernatural. Fanbury himself perceived this, for he suddenly said humbly, "All this is a little outside my experience. I mean—here!" He waved his hand round to indicate his quiet rural parish dreaming prosaically in the June sunlight. "But would you like me to pray—with you?"

Pelham remembered last night. "I *can't* pray—not even with you. I don't feel it'd be any use, and if I don't feel that, it wouldn't *be* any use, would it? And if, on top of that, *you* too don't really believe that it is someone—something not human…"

Fanbury bowed his head in acknowledgement. "I find it difficult. You see, here in this pleasant peaceful place, on this beautiful peaceful day such things not only seem very remote but, because of the very peace, lose their power. Now if only that peace could enter into you, you would find comfort, and then be able to pray. Come to our church tomorrow. A straightforward little country service among simple folk may give you…"

Pelham momentarily lost his temper, his nerves on edge from worry and lack of sleep. "It needs more than simple hymn-singing with a lot of countrymen to help me," he snapped.

Fanbury looked hurt and did not reply for a moment. Then he said gently, "Yes, I see. But I still don't know what I can do for you."

"I don't know either," said Pelham unhappily. "I just want help. It's all getting stronger, more invincible. A few weeks ago I was actually amused at the thought of having a double by chance in London. Now it's *the* Double, an uncanny overwhelming terror, lying in wait everywhere, growing into my life, like a—like a cancer." His voice choked suddenly and Fanbury laid an arm on his shoulders. He was on stronger ground here, for he had helped many parishioners through moments of misery and despair. He murmured soothing words till Pelham had collected himself once more.

"I want to know just *what* this is," he resumed.

"I—I'm afraid I'm only a simple clergyman…"

"But that's it. It's because you're a clergyman I came to you. I *know* now," he continued boldly, "that this is really an evil spirit…"

"But, but my dear fellow!" Faced at last with the bald statement, Fanbury looked both scandalized and frightened.

"Could it be the evil side of *me* suddenly taking shape, like a—a split personality becoming material? Fighting against the good side?"

"Good and evil are implanted in us; but they war within, not outside. I really can't accept…"

"But you must," cried Pelham urgently, "because that I'm now certain is the only way you can help."

"But, even admitting that… that—" He found he could not form the words. "What can I do?"

Pelham was silent a moment and asked tentatively: "Couldn't it be exorcised, or something like that?"

He could see Fanbury was quite shattered by this suggestion. He knew in that moment he should never have come. The man he had once known was gone, buried under conformity and ease and a gentle unexacting life from which all unconventional thought and ideas had long ago been excluded.

There's no set church service for that sort of thing," he hedged at last, "but occasionally priests make up a form of their own." He saw Pelham looking eagerly at him and went on: "For haunted houses and so on, I mean. But even that's rather outside my province. I've never even dreamed of…"

"Couldn't you try? To help me?"

Fanbury looked away, and Pelham guessed more or less what his reply would be. He was not far wrong. "I can't think what the Bishop would say."

"Never mind the Bishop! You are all priests of God. You believe that angels exist; in fact, you have to, don't you? Surely then you must admit there are evil spirits as well as good ones?"

"Certainly, I have a firm faith in the existence of angels. But…" He hesitated.

"But," Pelham echoed a little scornfully. Then: "I should have thought it was not possible fully to believe in God, unless one believed in Satan too."

"That is an—well…" Again he did not finish his sentence, merely dropped his eyes, looking extremely uncomfortable. An awkward silence fell and, when later it was broken, as if by consent they talked desultorily about other matters. Pelham knew that, like Travers and Dr Frazier, the other had failed him. Neither material, mental nor spiritual aid had been vouchsafed him.

"I'm so sorry I can't help you more," said Fanbury as they shook hands at the drive gate on departure. He was genuinely distressed at his inadequacy and at the misery in Pelham's eyes. He wished he could give him comfort but knew that all he could sincerely say was that he couldn't quite believe the story as related to him and that a spell in a nursing home would be the best thing. To suggest that, however, in the present circumstances would be cruel. He sighed unhappily as he watched the other start down the road to the village. Then on a sudden impulse he called him back. "I fear I have failed you badly. You realise I can't quite see this thing as you do. But if you do truly believe that this—this persecutor of you is an—is something evil…"

"I do."

"Then when you meet him, as I feel sure you must in time, make the sign of the Cross and say, 'In the name of the Father and the Son and the Holy Ghost I abjure you. Go back whence you came'."

"Thanks," said Pelham sincerely, and went on his way. It was a very small crumb of comfort in place of all that he had hoped, but it was at least something.

What he did that afternoon he only vaguely remembered. Foreseeing a weekend of long and helpful talks he had hired a car out from Newton Abbot that morning and booked a room in the small inn at Ossingford. But, not wanting to meet Fanbury again, he now cancelled it, returned to Newton Abbot and re-booked his previous night's accommodation. In the evening he found himself in the hotel bar, where he spent several hours, morose and solitary, avoiding entering into conversation with those about him and drinking whisky. But even that could not dispel his hopelessness.

Next morning he went to a church for the first time for many years and after listening to a good sermon, waited in the porch as the congregation slowly departed. But when he found himself alone with the clergyman, he changed his mind. There was a simple God-fearing honesty in the other's eyes, but was that enough? He could not see himself going through the same sort of conversation all over again.

He took a bus out into the countryside in the afternoon, wandered across some fields and came at last to a wood. Here he found an unexpected peace, as though the gracious oaks and beeches had beneficial powers of their own to keep evil influences at a distance. For the first time for some weeks he felt *safe*.

But the wood came to an abrupt end, and, crossing a small ride, he found himself entering a plantation of dark, pencil-like conifers, growing so close together that the sunlight could not penetrate and their lower branches were all dead and rotten, as were many smaller

145

trees which had succumbed earlier in the fight for survival. And here the atmosphere suddenly changed to an oppressive sense of malignity. The sombre close-packed tree-trunks prevented him seeing further than a few yards in any direction, as though deliberately screening hostile influences which were only waiting to close in on him. No birds sang; there was no colour, except the uniform dirty brown, shading slowly into muddy green high about his head.

Pelham shuddered, turned on his heel and swiftly retraced his steps as far as the ride. There was evil as well as good even in the trees of the countryside. He skirted round the menacing plantation and on the far side came upon open oak and beech once more. Walking through these he arrived at the cheerful normality of another main road with speeding cars, and a little way away a bus shelter at a crossroads.

From here he caught a bus back to Newton Abbot. That evil-looking plantation had given him an idea. Indeed, it had seemed symbolic. The pleasant peace of the first wood had been destroyed by those threatening trees, but he had run away from them and found it again. He could run away also from the Double who had demolished the pleasant peace of his life and perhaps recapture that too. Most of the latter's uncanny manoeuvring depended on Pelham being at hand, or rather on the *possibility* of his being where the Double himself chose to be. If he went away, right away, abroad, say to France or Italy, the Double would be in difficulties. There would be no object in following him out there, posing as him in a place where Pelham had no friends, no business, was not even known. And he could not stay behind carrying on his present interferences with the lives of others when Pelham had not only announced to everyone that he was going to France, but actually was in France in person, writing from there to Ed MacAndrew and his other friends, sending picture postcards to Lily or Paddy and instructions to Gough and Rogerson about forwarding letters, all the normal correspondence of a man on holiday... He could even take Rogerson with him and shut up the flat for several weeks—indeed that would be a very wise and necessary move—not to return till at last the Double had admitted defeat and—what was it Fanbury had said?—gone back whence he came.

Arrived at Newton Abbot, he packed and caught the next train to London, reaching Paddington at nine-thirty that night.

But it was with sudden apprehension that he let himself into his flat. Preoccupied with his plans for leaving England be had forgotten, till now, that he had returned from Devon a day earlier than he had said, for he had not originally intended to leave till Monday. Perhaps the Double had taken advantage of that and was even now, as he had been only three nights ago, again in his bedroom. The hall lights were not on, just as on that terrible night, though a gleam showed under Rogerson's door down the passage to the left indicating that he was preparing for bed.

Once inside, he stood still, wondering whether Rogerson had heard the key in the lock and at any moment would come out, to be dumbfounded at the sight of his master fully dressed and with suit-case when, just as before, he had supposed him to be in bed.

For some minutes he stayed there, hardly breathing, listening to the thudding of his heart. Fear was increasing in him and he jumped nervously at the sound of a wardrobe door being shut in Rogerson's room. The man had evidently not heard him come in. Pelham drew a deep breath, switched on the hall light and moved forward so that he could see down the other passage to his bedroom door. He began suddenly to feel physically sick with terror of the unknown. Was there actually anybody—any Thing—behind that door? Dared he walk forward and go calmly in like any other man entering his own bedroom? Or should he go along to Rogerson's room first and learn from his reaction what to expect?

The sick feeling passed. If it *was* an evil spirit, and he was there, then Fanbury had told him what to do. The sign of the Cross and the words of abjuration. He wondered suddenly whether they'd be any good. A mere formal phrase against a powerful and malevolent force of evil.

After a few moments he pulled himself together. Rogerson's presence would help. "Rogerson!" he called loudly.

After a short pause there came a startled, "Yes, what is it?" as though the other had not recognised his voice. Then, as he heard the sound of the opening door, he strode forward to his bedroom and laid his hand on the knob.

Rogerson was now in the hall. Pelham turned the handle, flung open the door and rapidly signing with his finger in the air began, "In the name of the Father, the…"

He stopped. The room was quite empty, the bed undisturbed; everything was exactly as it should have been.

Rogerson, coming up behind him, gave a sudden exclamation and whirling round Pelham saw the amazement on his face. His terror suddenly returned. The man was surprised to see the room empty and Pelham fully dressed. The Double *had* been there. Then relief flooded him as Rogerson explained, "I didn't expect you back till tomorrow."

"Oh, I—I remembered that I had a lot of things to do in the office on Monday," he managed to get out, still a little shaken.

To this after a considerable pause Rogerson merely replied, "Oh!" which was so unlike him that Pelham looked at him sharply. His previous remark, too, had not been his usual deferential manner of speaking and he had omitted his invariable "sir". What on earth was the matter with the fellow? Then a faint aroma of whisky reached his nostrils. With an enormous shock it dawned on him that Rogerson, the staid sober Rogerson, had been drinking. His eyes were slightly glazed, and Pelham could see that, dimly aware he had not behaved correctly, he was now trying to pull himself together and put it right.

"I regret, sir," he said laboriously. "I had not expected you back and was retiring for the night. Otherwise of course I would have turned your bed down, as is my…"

"Never mind that!" cut in Pelham, realising thankfully that in his present state the other had apparently not noticed anything extraordinary about his conduct at the bedroom door and he need not search for some plausible explanation. "Listen, Rogerson," he went on slowly, feeling he ought to tell him about his future plans as soon as possible whether he took it in properly or not. "I'm back early because I want to square up in the office tomorrow. I've decided, rather suddenly, to go abroad for a short holiday on the Continent the day after tomorrow."

Rogerson inclined his head with extreme gravity. "Very good, sir."

"And I think you'd better go to bed," he said coldly.

Evidently not trusting further speech, Rogerson inclined his head again, and with careful dignity retired down the passage.

18

Rogerson, entirely master of himself and urbane as ever, met Pelham's eye at breakfast next morning without a trace of embarrassment or guilt, as though he was suggesting in his own way that the matter might be forgotten. It wouldn't be surprising, thought Pelham, if he actually had forgotten the whole interlude, for he'd certainly been very drunk; but later he made some reference to his master's intended holiday, which showed he had not; so Pelham himself decided to ignore it. After all, he reasoned, one lapse in five years was not a very great matter. Maybe Rogerson had had some bad news and gone out and bought himself a bottle of whisky—Pelham was positive he would not have touched his master's—to help him forget it. And in a way it was partly his own fault for coming back early without warning. Besides, he simply couldn't be bothered with any domestic contretemps when he had to make his plans for going away.

He took a taxi all the way to the office to save time, and as soon as he arrived sent the office boy out for a B.E.A. timetable. He had decided to go by air; he wanted to find himself out of England as quickly as possible with one swift break. The timetable too would give him an idea of where to go, about which he had not made up his mind. Somewhere not too far away, he felt, so that he could have an early breakfast before starting and yet be wherever it was in time for lunch. Once he'd settled on a destination, he could ring Thomas Cook's, book his seat, get them to fix hotel accommodation, and then go round and collect the ticket on his way home at the end of the afternoon. Meanwhile a day's hard work in the office with Lily Clement and Danvers should suffice to organize things for smooth running during his absence.

Anxious to get busy on this last, he was rather annoyed to find that Lily did not answer his bell and was not in her little room. She had apparently chosen this particular morning to be late for work. While waiting for her to arrive, he rang Ed Travers's office, and—Ed being

149

still on holiday—left a message that he was going abroad next day. He then phoned MacAndrew and several other acquaintances and business associates to the same effect, and he also told Gough at the Savernake Club, saying he'd let him know later where to forward any letters. The more people who knew of his intention the more difficult, if not impossible, it would make it for the Double to try anything on during his absence.

Lily still not having turned up, he next had Danvers in and broke the news to him. The old man looked a little startled: his employer had never done anything like that before at such short notice; but then these last weeks he hadn't known rightly what to make of Mr Pelham—working like a beaver for a day or so here and there, down in the dumps the rest of the time, popping in and out, wearing unusual clothes. Privately, he considered it high time he did get away for a bit.

"As soon as Miss Clement comes in, Danvers," Pelham went on, "we'll start making the necessary office arrangements for my absence. What can have happened to her, by the way? It's well past ten."

"But you gave her permission to be late, sir. You told me she'd asked for a long weekend, you remember, and you let her go on Friday afternoon."

"Oh yes, of course," replied Pelham hastily. He had forgotten that the Double would almost certainly have visited the office again during his absence. The horrible fear of the evil being whom he knew could not be really human began to return—even though he realised that by midday tomorrow he would be miles away, out of danger.

"Ah, here is Miss Clement now, sir," said Danvers as the door opened, and Lily walked in. With a cheerful "Good morning" to the two men she crossed to her room, adding to Pelham as she went: "I do hope I'm not *too* late?"

"No, that's all right. Did you enjoy your weekend?"

Lily hesitated a brief moment, then "Very much, thanks," she replied politely and went out, to return a moment later with pencil and pad ready for work.

"We are going to be busy, Miss Clement," Danvers told her. "Mr Pelham is starting on a holiday tomorrow. Short notice," he smiled, "but I expect the office can cope."

"I'm sure it can, Mr Danvers."

"Well," said Pelham briskly. "Let's get things organized. Danvers, will you bring in any files and so on out there which you think will need attention during my absence!"

As soon as Danvers was out of the room, Lily began to laugh softly.

"What's the joke, Lily?"

"Everything!" she replied happily. "But principally you and me and Danvers just now. Oh, so formal and natural!"

"But what…"

"And when you asked if I'd enjoyed my weekend, I could hardly keep my face straight."

"I don't see what was funny about that. It was a perfectly sincere question."

Lily grew suddenly grave, though her eyes were dancing. She came forward to the desk and leaned on it looking straight at him.

"Then I'll give you a perfectly sincere answer. I enjoyed every minute of it more than I've enjoyed anything ever before. I'm so happy and content, and life's too lovely for words."

Pelham felt his mouth falling open. He could not imagine what had happened to her. She was an entirely different girl. Obviously brimming with happiness, she looked just as she had said—content, satisfied, almost sleek; like a cat that had had a large saucer of cream. Indeed, she did seem a little like a cat, Pelham thought suddenly; he had never noticed it before.

He was just about to speak when there was a knock at the door and the office boy came in with the B.E.A. timetable.

"Thanks," said Pelham, taking it, a little annoyed to observe that Lily had quickly whipped up her pad and pencil and assumed the attitude of a secretary taking a letter—rather guiltily, he thought.

He put the folder on his desk and got up. "Now, what *is* all this, Lily?"

She only pouted. "Why the Lily? It was to be 'Lilith' between us, wasn't it? I love it—your own special name for me."

"Lilith! I've never…" He checked, the cold fear stealing over him again. *What* had the Double been doing?

"It was Lilith yesterday and the day before." Her voice was husky, low and sensuous. "And that wonderful Friday night when you first invented it for me."

Pelham stood staring at her. At last the awful unbelievable truth had dawned on him.

"I—I…" he began.

But with a swift movement Lily had stopped his mouth with half-parted, passionately clinging lips and then was whispering fervently in his ear. "Oh, darling, you were so wonderful and sweet and clever and I just adore you."

Like a man in a dream Pelham disengaged himself, heard himself saying stupidly: "This—this is… In the office, too… Anyone might…"

Lily also drew quickly away, contrite. "I'm sorry. You're quite right. I forgot it's the office. But it's you who've made me forget everything except…"

"Lily!" Pelham cut in in a shaking voice. "Please leave me at once. I've—I've got things to think about… I'll—I'll call you when I want you."

"I understand. I *am* sorry." Submissively she went to the door. Turning, she flashed him a meaning little smile of shared intimacy and disappeared.

Pelham almost tottered to his chair and slumped down, hands limp on the desk before him. This was terrible. He felt himself curling up inside at the memory of the recent scene and its implications. Lily and the Double—the Double who was not of this world, but was…

He jerked himself upright. He couldn't face his thoughts, couldn't face anything. He must get away as soon as possible, at once. He couldn't now stay in London, in England, a moment longer than he had to.

He snatched at the timetable on the desk, his brain busy in a dozen directions at once. Rogerson could pack a bag for him and bring it down to the Air Station—he must tell him to be sure and remember his passport—just clothes for the first few days would do—he could have further luggage sent after him—better still, Rogerson could join him with it abroad in a few days' time—let's see, twenty to eleven now—it shouldn't take the fellow more than half an hour to pack—

allow another half-hour for taxiing down—he could be off any time after, say, eleven-forty-five.

With trembling fingers he was already leafing through the booklet. Brussels, Copenhagen, Madrid, it didn't matter as long as it was a plane he could catch as soon as… Ah! here was one—Amsterdam, depart London, Waterloo Air Terminal, 1150 hours…

He thrust the timetable away and grabbed the phone. Warn Rogerson to get busy first, then off to Waterloo—he could get his ticket there—and wait for Rogerson. He'd have time, too, while waiting, to phone Lily and say he'd been called away suddenly… No, he was forgetting, he simply couldn't do that, not after what had passed… He'd tell Danvers instead.

He had now finished dialling the number and was listening to the distant ringing, visualising Rogerson stopping his dusting or bed-making or whatever he was doing and coming to the phone. He was going to be considerably startled, Pelham realised, but he was well trained enough not to argue and to carry out his instructions quickly and accurately.

He heard the receiver being lifted, but before Rogerson could announce the number with his usual grave politeness, Pelham was talking rapidly.

"Rogerson, I've had to change my plans and I'm in a great hurry. Will you pack a large suit-case at once and…"

A voice which was not Rogerson's but yet was faintly familiar here interrupted him. "I think you have the wrong number. This is Maida Vale 50732."

"I'm so sorry…" he began automatically, then broke off. That *was* his number. "But that isn't Rogerson, surely?"

"No, this is Mr Pelham."

The room seemed to turn over. A sudden icy sweat broke out all over him. In a moment, his palms were slippery with it and he almost dropped the receiver. It was the Double himself answering. He clutched the edge of the desk with his free hand and tried to form words but could not.

"This is Mr Pelham speaking," the other was repeating. "Who is it, please?"

He pulled himself together, beat back the waves of terror which were engulfing him. "No, no," he shouted. "*This* is Mr Pelham. I'm phoning from my own office to my own flat. Who—who are *you*?"

"I've told you." The voice now held exactly the same friendly amusement, faintly superior, as his own would have done in similar circumstances. "Your name may be Pelham too, of course, and it's certainly quite a coincidence that your wrong number should produce another one of us—but I'm J. M. Pelham of Pelham Lake and Co., Bedford Street, and Flat 10, Clitheroe Court."

Pelham changed the receiver to the other hand and wiped his clammy palm on his trousers. "I haven't got a wrong number."

"Then what can I do for you?" was the courteous reply.

Yes, Pelham reflected with half his mind, that was exactly what he would have said and exactly how he would have said it. "I—I want to speak to Rogerson," he got out desperately. Surely, he could convince Rogerson that he was the real Mr Pelham, who had barely a couple of hours ago left his flat for a busy day at the office and would never have suddenly returned without a good reason. But then, his heart sank, the Double would have had some plausible explanation.

"My manservant? Is it important?" The voice was now a little curt. "Because I've told him he's not supposed to be rung up on my phone by his friends."

Again just what he himself would have replied: indeed those were his instructions. "It's not important," he said dully. How could Rogerson accept the mere word of someone on the phone, with his master obviously there beside him in the flesh? He had a brainwave. "In fact, it doesn't matter. It was merely to say I'm going abroad today—at once. I apologise for bothering you."

"That's all right. I'll give him the message," he just heard the other reply as he put the receiver down and jumped up. But he knew the message would certainly not be given. Nor did he care. He had said that purposely to put his enemy off the scent. He was not going abroad at once. He was going to make one last effort to confront and beat his adversary. For the terror had suddenly left him towards the end of the conversation: The Double had been so like him, amused, friendly, polite, but no longer inspiring fear any more than he himself would have done.

And there was another thing. However like him the Double might be in appearance and manner, his voice was not quite right. Each phrase and intonation was perfectly imitated, but the timbre, the basic quality of the voice, had been slightly wrong throughout; otherwise, Pelham knew, he would have recognised it at once as his own. And though Rogerson could be deceived by a voice so exactly similar when his master was not there, he would certainly know the difference when they were both together.

He grabbed his hat and umbrella. He was once more angry, aggressive, and above all confident that an immediate showdown for which he had been so long striving—would result in victory. And the Double was only a twenty-minute taxi ride away—and not expecting him. He would meet him, and win.

He slipped out of the door just a second before Danvers came in with an armful of files from the outer office.

155

19

P elham sat forward on the edge of the taxi seat willing it to go faster. This time the Double would not elude him. After what he had said on the phone, his swift arrival at the flat, he felt sure, would be quite unforeseen, and once inside he would not move from the hall. Escape would be impossible—unless the Double vanished into thin air. The thought sobered him: convinced though he was that in some mysterious way his enemy was not really human he hadn't yet fully considered all the implications. But he quickly put that idea out of his mind, grimly reflecting that if it did happen it would at least solve his problem. Strangely enough he still felt no fear, at least nothing comparable with the overwhelming terror that had descended upon him the previous Thursday night and had gripped him again at intervals up to ten minutes ago when he had actually spoken to the other on the telephone.

And now the opportunity for which he had been seeking all these weeks had come. The Double would have to leave him alone and go out of his life when the impersonation was really exposed. For Rogerson, who had known him all these years, would see them side by side, would above all hear them speak, could even, if he wanted, ask them test questions. He wished now he had chosen that particular morning to wear the unusual ready-made suit and pale brown hat, which Rogerson hated so much; for while the Double might easily be dressed in the same sort of clothes as he now wore, he would hardly have thought of those, or been able to obtain similar ones. But at the time his intention had been to escape utterly from all thought or possible contact with him; he had not envisaged this impending encounter in which he would need every... Wait! There was the tie! The red-and-green tie he'd been carrying about for days for just such an occasion. Not another like it, the man in the shop had said. He plunged a hand into his pocket. Thank Heaven he had the little parcel on him still. Swiftly he stripped off his normal dark tie and substituted the other. That could well be the deciding factor, he thought, and smiled almost happily to himself.

He paid the taxi off, went up to his flat and paused outside the door listening. There was no sound from within. He prayed that the Double was still there and—he hadn't thought of such a disastrous possibility till now—that Rogerson hadn't gone out to do the morning's shopping.

He took a deep breath; then very quietly he let himself in, closed the door behind him, and advanced a couple of paces into the hall. With enormous relief he heard the whirr of a carpet-sweeper in his bedroom. So Rogerson was in.

He wondered whether he should call him but remembered he had done that only the night before—and the Double had not been there after all. It occurred suddenly to him that the same thing might have happened: he might not be there now, might have guessed his intention. Well, in that case he still had his original plan.

Rogerson could pack a suitcase and he'd go straight down to the Air Terminal. Meanwhile he stayed quiet and awaited developments.

After a few minutes Rogerson emerged, propped the sweeper against the wall, and came down the passage. He was right in the hall before he saw Pelham standing there with his hat on, obviously having come in from outside. His jaw dropped; he threw a swift glance at the sitting-room door. "Why, sir, I could have sworn…" he began, and suddenly his control snapped. "What *is* the matter with you these days? Going out and coming in every half-hour without my…" He pulled himself up. "I *beg* your pardon, sir. I fully believed you to be still in the sitting-room reading the paper."

"No, no," said Pelham excitedly. "The man in there isn't me. That's the whole trouble. He's an impostor. It's been going on for…" He noticed Rogerson was just staring at him blankly, and tried to speak more slowly and reasonably, forcing a smile. "It's all right. Don't be alarmed. This is me—here. And as for that fellow, I'm going to…"

The door of the sitting-room opened. A man came out.

Mr Pelham stood transfixed. He just could not believe it. It was like looking at himself in a mirror—little moustache, pleasant roundish face, neatly brushed hair, kindly eyes, clothes exactly the same. But—and he noticed this with triumph—the other was wearing a dark tie just like

157

Pelham usually wore—not the new flamboyant one he had donned in the taxi.

There was a silence broken only by Rogerson. "Christ Almighty!" he ejaculated and began to edge away.

"Don't go, Rogerson!" said the other in Pelham's friendly tones. "I think I shall need your help in this matter." Rogerson paused, still looked dazedly from one to the other.

Pelham regained his composure. Whatever he really was, the figure in front of him seemed just an ordinary person; he must fight him on his own ground and he knew he would win. He opened his mouth, but the other was before him, still addressing Rogerson.

"You may have noticed I've been very much worried these last days, not quite myself in fact?" Rogerson gulped and nodded dumbly. "Well, this man is the cause of it all." He turned to Pelham. "I'm glad you've put in a real appearance at last."

Would he have said just that? Pelham found himself vaguely wondering. Yes, he would, given the same circumstances. But the Double was continuing: "You've been pestering me for some time, because of your likeness to me, and honestly I'm tired of it." He turned to Rogerson again. "I didn't tell you at the time, but I have reason to think this man actually got into the flat here on one occasion—you might have noticed that I—or rather he—probably didn't behave in my usual manner?" Rogerson, still speechless, nodded again.

"But that's not true." Pelham suddenly found he was almost shouting. And it was very unlike him to shout. It didn't help his case. He should be quieter, more restrained. Like, indeed, the other Mr Pelham was now, as he continued, "That's why I had the lock changed."

"Ah yes, of course, sir," Rogerson stammered.

Pelham gasped. That "sir" to the wrong man. "Rogerson! You know me, don't you? You know my voice. Can't you see that though he's speaking like me his voice is different?"

Rogerson shook his head. "You sound dead alike," he muttered.

"But…" Too late Pelham now remembered once being told by a radio actor that one could never, when speaking, hear one's own voice exactly as it sounded to others, something to do with resonance in the skull. So the Double even had the same voice after all. "Oh, never mind that then! Surely you know *me*? You've been with me five years; don't you *know* me?" he finished almost imploringly.

"Go on, Rogerson!" said the other in Mr Pelham's own level tones. "Answer him!"

Rogerson was still almost too shattered to speak by a situation outside all his previous experience. And when words at last burst out of him, he spoke for once as himself and not as a trained manservant.

"Well it's Gawd's truth, I never set eyes on a pair so alike in all my natural. No one would believe me if I was to tell 'em. The hair, eyes, faces of both of you. If you was to put me on my dying oath I couldn't answer. But I'd swear to each of you separate."

Pelham's heart suddenly sank. Till that moment he had thought that Rogerson would, must, could not help recognizing him in spite of everything.

"But, Rogerson," he cried. "Think of all the things we've done together, talked about, before the—this…"

"Don't shout so loud. No good can come of shouting!" It was a stock phrase of Pelham's and he saw Rogerson's recognition of it as he looked quickly at the speaker. "Well, let's think of some things, shall we?" His eyes flickered towards Pelham and now he noticed that they had become cold, hard, hostile. Had *he* ever looked like that? he wondered miserably, but the other was continuing: "You remember a few nights ago, Rogerson, when I went to the pictures and you left supper out for me?"

"Yes, sir. Most certainly. The night you weren't well, had a bad dream and forgot you…"

"But it wasn't—" began Pelham and was silent. He couldn't say he wasn't there.

The other turned back to him. "Just repeat to Rogerson what his master said to him when he poured out the first glass of hock."

"But it was you who were…" Pelham started and again stopped.

"The very point I'm making," smiled the other. "Well, I said, 'It's really a shame to drink it: there are only nine bottles left'." He turned to Rogerson who mutely nodded confirmation. "You see, he doesn't know—naturally." He turned again to Pelham. "And then Rogerson said—what?"

Pelham again tried to speak but found nothing to say. He felt like a rat in a trap. The other's gaze was colder, more hostile. A little flicker of fear began to rise in him.

"You see again! Very well then, I'll tell you. What Rogerson said was, 'Only eight now, sir—this one's as good as gone'."

"That's right," cut in Rogerson, all at once himself again. "You're Mr Pelham all right, sir. But Gawd's truth, he's like you."

"I'm not. I'm not. It's him who's like *me*. He's sapping my life. He's…"

"Be quiet, you!" Against his volition Pelham stopped. "One last point, Rogerson. He's done something even more silly than coming here today, when he assumed I was at the office. Did you ever see me wearing a tie like that thing?"

"But I bought it ten days ago!" Pelham's voice was shrill with frustration and increasing fear. "It's to prove that…"

"No, sir, never," answered Rogerson ignoring him. "You haven't got a tie like that and you'd *never* have bought one."

"Exactly. Remember all this, will you? It will be important later in the witness-box. Thank you, Rogerson, that'll do now."

Shaking his head and with an angry contemptuous glance at his real master, the manservant went along to his quarters. And with him it seemed to little Mr Pelham went all light and life and security. He turned to the other and suddenly saw that the face had changed. From it, from his whole being, there came waves of malignancy, of terrible power, of something that was not human for all its human shape.

"You did make a mistake about that tie, didn't you?" he said in quite a new voice, a steely impersonal tone which seemed to slice through Pelham's brain. "I could have been wearing it too; but I didn't, because it gave me a nice chance."

"But why"—it was almost a whisper—"why have you done this to me?"

His question was not answered. "At last," cried the other, with firm evil exultancy, "I am truly *here*; and what a future is mine! What can't I do?" He seemed to lick his lips. "Indeed, I haven't done badly already.

160

Jack Benton, Tom Clement, little Lilith. Rogerson also incidentally; he's begun to drink secretly—stealing your whisky too, or I should say mine. He won't last with me long: I shall have to sack him without a character when I come back from abroad—and find out. He'll go nicely downhill after that."

Pelham found he had been bleating ineffectual interruptions during this. "But you can't, you can't," he now got out, and suddenly remembered something. The waves of terror, of a thick clammy fear that could only come from the other world, were beating relentlessly over him, but he raised his right hand, forced his trembling lips to speak. "In the name of..."

"In the devil's name what are you playing at?" swiftly cut in the other's harsh metallic voice. "Threatening me? Well, I'm calling Rogerson and you're going to be given in charge for impersonation."

"No, no," cried Pelham, his hand dropping feebly to his side. "Let me go away. You must..." He advanced imploringly upon the figure in front of him and suddenly reeled as if against an invisible barrier.

"Who—who are you?" he croaked piteously.

The other looked pleasantly at him for a moment, all hostility gone. There was only kind tolerance in his voice as he replied in Pelham's normal voice:

"Why, Mr Pelham of course. J. M. Pelham."

It was then that Pelham started screaming.

20

"What *was* the strange case, Captain Masters?" asked Joanna.

"Yes, the unnerving experience Mr Pelham had?" added David.

"Well!" Masters stroked his heavy moustache. "It seems by some coincidence that there was a fella knocking about London who was exactly like him in appearance."

"You mean an absolute double of him?"

"Spitting image, I gather. And the chap apparently discovered the likeness and started cashing in on it. I don't know the details—probably ran up bills and borrowed money and so forth. And then I suppose he had the bright idea of somethin' bigger. So he actually went to Jim Pelham's flat—it was before he moved to his Dorchester House suite, of course—apparently aiming to put his act across on the manservant and clean up any valuables lying around."

"But what a risk to take! Surely Mr Pelham's own manservant couldn't be fooled?"

"We-ell, I don't know; I believe the likeness was quite uncanny. But as it happened, though Jim Pelham had started off to his office as usual, he came back for some reason and so was at the flat when the fella called. Of course, that blew the whole game sky-high. There was rather a terrifying scene, and in the middle of it the man suddenly went clean off his rocker, right in front of Jim Pelham. Horrible business. Screamin' and clawin' and frothin', y'know. He and his man had the hell of a fight before they could tie him up and get the police along."

"How awful!" Joanna shuddered sympathetically.

"Of course, the chap must have been half crackers to start with. Anyway, he's safely tucked away in an asylum. Quite crazy, and really believing now that he *is* Jim Pelham and that the real one isn't. Somethin' rather ironic in that somewhere if you see what I mean."

"And that's what changed Mr Pelham, as you were saying just now?"

162

"Apparently. He went abroad for a holiday and when he came back, he was different. Dynamic. Go-ahead. Quite a business ball of fire. How he'd kept all that brain and energy under before I don't know."

"Oh dear!" exclaimed Joanna suddenly. One of the old ladies behind whose chairs they had been hopefully waiting had got up to go and before David could move a hard-faced girl with a curt "*Pardon!*" had slipped in. "We've missed it. My husband feels he won't have luck tonight unless he sits," she explained to Captain Masters.

"Come down to the other end then," he suggested. "There are fewer people standing there, so you should have a chance soon."

"Yes and you'll be able to see Mr Pelham close up," put in Fred Dyson who'd just rejoined them. He had broken away a few moments before to talk to a girl he knew. "Mollie Johnson there and I are off to the bar. Bye-bye! See you before you go tomorrow," he added wickedly.

He left them and they moved down to the other half of the double table where they found themselves now right opposite the object of their interest. Masters drew some plaques from his pocket and tossed one on red over the shoulder of those seated.

While Joanna watched Mr Pelham, David studied the girl. She certainly was, as he had earlier decided from a distance, highly attractive—sensuous and unconsciously provocative. No wonder all the men in the neighbourhood kept covertly looking at her, irresistibly drawn like flies to honey. Then a moment later her gaze casually met his, and he experienced a sudden near-shock, as though unexpectedly shown something deliciously tempting—and yet harmful. Her eyes were quite impersonal—she was merely glancing idly round the table—yet the physical allure in them was overwhelmingly there.

He forced himself to stop looking and turned his gaze to Mr Pelham. How commonplace he seemed in his person—even close to—yet with so much latent power and self-assurance. At that moment the other glanced up, recognised Masters and smiled briefly, extending his smile to embrace David and Joanna when he saw they were with him. Captain Masters gave a little wave in return, picked up some small winnings that the croupier had just pushed across to him and went round the table end to talk briefly with Mr Pelham.

Joanna was nudging David, whispering, "I see what Fred meant about his eyes. So ordinary; and then just for a moment—not ordinary at all." She gave a little shiver. "Not by any means."

"I know," returned David. He too had been quite startled by a momentary strange quality in the other's gaze. It was inviting—as though he had seen and known everything in the world and wanted to put his knowledge at the disposal of others—and yet it held an eerie quality of compulsion which was almost frightening.

"She's awfully well got up," remarked Joanna suddenly, off at a feminine tangent. "That hair goes beautifully with the emeralds."

"She's pretty terrific all round," said David, remembering her eyes.

"Darling! I shall have to watch you, I can see."

"She's *his* secretary, not mine. At least, that's what Fred said she was. He turned to Masters who had just rejoined them. "Who exactly is the girl with Mr Pelham?"

"Well, she's his secretary." He paused meaningly before the word, then dropped his voice for David's ear. "She's pretty hot stuff, too, between you and me. Likes the men, if y'know what I mean." He stroked his moustache with considerable complacency.

"But doesn't he..."

"Doesn't seem to mind."

"What's all this secret talk?" interrupted Joanna; and quickly David replied: "Just discussing Mr Pelham's secretary."

"I shouldn't have thought there was much secret about her."

"Meaning, darling?"

"Meaning I'm old enough to know secretaries aren't usually taken to Monte Carlo just to do stenography."

Masters looked a little embarrassed and went on quickly: "She had a bit of a rotten experience, too, about the same time."

"How?"

"It was discovered that her fiancé—who was a trusted confidential clerk with some company or other—had approached Pelham and offered to sell some of his firm's secrets."

"Oh, that *is* rather awful."

"Yes. I think Jim Pelham wanted to keep it from her, but he had to tell the young scoundrel's employers. They of course gave him the sack, and then he had the nerve to accuse Pelham of having bribed him to do it. So naturally the whole thing had to come into court and both she and Pelham had to give evidence. He ended up by going to prison, I believe."

"How rotten for her, poor girl!"

"I don't think she needs your sympathy now. You can see she's got over it." He laughed and jerked his head towards the table where the girl, smiling happily at her companion, was sweeping some plaques into her bag.

"Oh look! I think she's getting up. David! Go round quick! Oh, too late!"

A man had begun to take the vacant seat, but another young man in a dinner-jacket, who had been standing behind Mr Pelham's chair, rather aggressively edged him out of it and sat down himself.

"That's all right," said Masters cheerfully. "All arranged. Pelham was asking about you just now and I told him you were waiting for a place. Come along."

"But the seat's gone."

"Only to Jim Pelham's young man. Goes about everywhere with him. Sort of manservant and general companion type. A tough one too. Might almost be called a bodyguard. He's the girl's brother, incidentally."

"Oh!" Joanna was a little shocked. "Isn't that rather... With his sister being—well, you know. It doesn't sound very nice."

"He does well out of the arrangement and his morals are his own affair."

They had by now moved round and introductions were made. Joanna felt a queer little tremor as she shook hands with Mr Pelham. And that was funny, she thought, because it wasn't as though he was a blond handsome young demi-god, which might have excused any woman, even a happily married one, from feeling a faint thrill. In fact it wasn't that sort of thrill at all. It was more like... But then she was being introduced to the girl who smiled into her eyes with a peculiar welcoming look, which yet was too impersonal to be a genuinely friendly welcome. It had hunger in it, like a cat waiting for a bird to... An absurd thought: she checked herself. But they were strange people,

165

particularly the man. Fred had said earlier that they were the queerest pair he had ever met, and she found herself wholeheartedly agreeing. Glancing sideways at David she could see he was thinking much the same.

"I hear you feel you can't win tonight unless you sit down," Mr Pelham was saying.

"Well, I don't suppose it matters really."

"Oh, but it does," put in the girl. "Luck's such a funny thing that you're most probably right." Her voice was low and slightly husky. "Come on, Tom," she added to the large young man who at once got up and politely offered Joanna his seat.

"No, it's David's hunch," Joanna said, just a little sharply. For some reason she didn't want him to stand behind with the girl. "David!"

Her husband jumped and turned to her. As he had briefly held the girl's warm hand in his and had looked, for the second time and now close to, into her eyes he had glimpsed active desire; and more, a suggestion of accessibility. "Pretty hot stuff—likes the men," Masters had said only a few minutes before; and he angrily checked an unbidden stirring of his blood. Strange phrases from somewhere or other came leaping to his mind. "The sweet seduction of sin" and then "temptress eternal yet incarnate". Really, he thought, and stole an almost shamefaced look at his young wife, at which a faint smile had curved the girl's full lips. Another phrase suddenly found its way into his brain—wasn't it a book of poems by some French author? "*Fleurs du Mal.*" That somehow seemed to hit her off: A Flower of Evil.

Joanna's voice here broke into his thoughts and with an effort he wrenched his gaze away, sat down abruptly and piled his store of plaques on the green baize.

"Are you here for long?" asked Mr Pelham.

"Well, I don't know, sir. Depends on that." He nodded towards the skittering ball, as the croupier intoned, "*Rien ne va plus!*"

"Ah, I see," laughed the other. "May I hope it will be over Friday?"

"Why?"

"I'm giving a little party on my yacht that evening. Perhaps you and your wife would come. I like to have young people around, and it'll be fun, I promise you."

He had leaned back including Joanna in the conversation and she promptly replied: "Oh, that'd be lovely! Thanks so much!" and David echoed her equally enthusiastically. "We've got to win now, darling," she went on, leaning over with her hands on his shoulders.

"*Faites vos jeux!*" droned the croupier.

"Take it easy at first," suggested Mr Pelham kindly. "Try the middle column and the *Passe*. But *don't* be stingy!"

David hesitated a moment, but there had seemed such confidence, even authority in the other's voice that he did as he was told with over half of the money in front of him, which made Joanna gasp and tighten her grip on his shoulders.

"By golly!" he said delightedly a few moments later. In that short space of time he had won about twelve thousand francs. "That was a good tip of yours, sir. You should have taken it yourself." For Mr Pelham had staked modestly on red and lost. "Any more where that came from?"

The other was watching him curiously. "No, it's your own hunch you must follow now."

David played two more rounds and lost. Then he won a small amount and then lost heavily, Mr Pelham watching him all the time. Soon he had only three thousand francs left.

"Oh, David!" Joanna almost wailed. "I don't *want* to go home tomorrow."

"Put it all on one number, it's the only thing now," advised Mr Pelham. "That'll give you about a hundred thousand francs."

"Yes, yes," muttered David. It would—if he won. But if he lost... Poor Joanna, he was thinking. We shouldn't have come in after all. "But I wonder which. I can't feel anything. My hunch seems to have vanished. What about you, darling?"

But, looking a little unhappy, Joanna only shook her head.

"We're all right for getting home and the hotel bill," he reassured her in an undertone.

"Try your age," suggested Mr Pelham. "Assuming, of course," he smiled, "you aren't over thirty-six."

"Yes, twenty-five!" urged Joanna, then suddenly the girl said in his ear, "I'll give you a lead." She threw a plaque casually on the table. It

167

fell practically *à cheval*, thirty-two and thirty-five. One of the croupiers looked up inquiringly. She nodded, and he tidied it more accurately into position with the corner of his rake.

"There!" she said. "Two chances instead of one." David hesitated a moment, then just before the "*Rien ne va plus*" he pushed his money up next hers.

Twenty-five came up.

Oh!" gasped Joanna heartbrokenly; then quickly collected herself, and added with forced lightness, "Well, we've had it! Home tomorrow!"

Mr Pelham had turned to look at the girl behind. "Really, Lilith!" he said, quite annoyed. "That's your fault! Your luck's been rotten all evening and now you've spoilt his."

She looked deep into David's eyes. "I'm so sorry," she murmured in her husky voice.

"It's all right. I'm only sorry we must miss your party."

"Oh dear, yes," cried Joanna, trying to be brave. "It was awfully nice of you to ask us, and I did so want…"

But Mr Pelham had dived into his pocket and produced a plaque for ten thousand francs which he slid in front of David. "Don't go yet, young man. One last try with this!"

"But I can't possibly…"

"Of course not," put in Joanna. "It's our own silly fault."

"No, it was this stupid young woman of mine. I feel responsible. And it's only a loan."

"But we couldn't pay it back if we lose. Or could we?" he added to Joanna.

She knew at once he was thinking of the money for the hotel bill of which she had earlier possessed herself. Only over her dead body, she had said at the time, well aware of her husband's weakness. "No darling," she said firmly. "We've got exactly enough for the hotel and no more."

"But," said Mr Pelham, "do you mean you really can't *afford* it? It's only a tenner, you know."

"Oh *that's* all right. We're not on the breadline at home. I simply mean our currency allowance has run out."

"Well, write me a cheque, my dear fellow."

"But it can't be cashed out here."

"There are ways," smiled Mr Pelham.

"It's not allowed…" began David, but Lilith suddenly interrupted, laying her hand on his shoulder. "Oh, but everyone knows that's all silly nonsense. I shall feel terrible if you don't accept."

David looked for a moment at Joanna. She met his eyes, glanced away deliberately, then said slowly: "I don't see that it really matters, does it?"

"And I'm the guilty one," murmured the husky voice penitently, and the hand on his shoulder tightened. "Because I made you lose."

Swiftly David wrote the cheque and gave it to Mr Pelham who, about to put it in his wallet, seemed to remember something and instead passed it to the young man behind his chair. "You may just catch Glinski with this, Tom," he said, "and he can put it through with that other one. I expect he's still in the bar."

"Okey-doke," said Tom. "Back in a jiff!"

"Now," said Mr Pelham turning back to David, "you must ensure in one swift motion that I have the pleasure of your company on Friday. Got a hunch?"

"Absolutely nothing, sir."

A turn was just spinning to a close and the croupier was announcing: "*Numéro treize, noir, impair et manque.*"

"Put it *en plein* on thirteen," ordered Mr Pelham, "and see what happens."

"But thirteen's just won."

"The chances for and against are still exactly the same for next time. Aren't they, Lilith?"

"You always say so, but I don't see why."

"And it's an unlucky number too." David was still doubtful.

"Not for some people. Try and see!"

David looked round at Joanna. Lips parted she nodded excitedly: already in her mind it had won. Then he looked at Mr Pelham and lastly at the girl. He felt quite strange—almost as though he had no option.

He slid the plaque forward—on to thirteen.

A little murmur went up from the table as a minute later the croupier announced that thirteen had won again. He pushed a stack of plaques across to David.

"Oh! Darling!" gabbled Joanna feverishly. "That's an enormous amount. Why, it's…"

"About three hundred and fifty pounds," laughed Mr Pelham. "Should last you a little longer than tomorrow."

"Why, we can even buy things…" Joanna fell suddenly silent in rapturous anticipation.

"Here, I can pay you back." David selected a ten-thousand plaque from his winnings and looked over his shoulder for the young man to whom Mr Pelham had given his cheque.

"I'm sorry but it's too late. It's on the moving belt." He smiled into David's eyes. "To tell you the truth I had no idea I was going to give you such good advice. Of course thirteen's *my* lucky number, but I didn't know it was going to be yours as well."

"It certainly was. And I really must thank you most awfully for lending me that…"

"Nonsense. It was really selfishness on my part. You see, I very much want you both to come to my party."

Appendix

Here follows a transcript of Anthony Armstrong's obituary as it appeared in The Times on 11th February 1976.

Anthony Armstrong: Author and playwright

Mr. Anthony Armstrong Willis, OBE, MC, the author and playwright, who was widely known under his nom de plume of Anthony Armstrong, died yesterday at the age of 79.

His reputation as a humorous writer was first made under the initials "A.A." familiar indeed in the 1920s and 1930s to readers of Punch. He also became known to the public as the author of a number of books which were for the most part either in his lighter vein or were crime novels. His plays, a good few of which were produced in London and of which perhaps the best known is Ten Minute Alibi, fell into the same two categories. Versatile, witty and ingenious he provided a great deal of excellent entertainment in his day.

Anthony Armstrong Willis was born on January 2, 1897, the elder son of Paymaster Captain G.H.A. Willis, CB, RN. Educated at Uppingham School and at Trinity College, Cambridge, he entered the Royal Engineers in 1915 and from 1916 to 1919 served with the 34th Division in France. Rising to the rank of Captain he was wounded, mentioned in dispatches, and awarded the MC. In 1925 he retired to the Regular Army Reserve. Shortly before this he had begun to write for Punch and until 1933 he was a weekly contributor to it. He also wrote for the New Yorker, Strand and other periodicals.

In 1939 he was invalided out of the reserve and in 1940 was commissioned as a squadron leader in the RAFVR to become founder and editor of Tee Emm, the RAF Training Memorandum. In this well-loved publication were recounted the adventures, or rather misadventures of Pilot Officer Prune as awful warnings to those who forgot their flying drill. For egregious blunders brought to the editor's

171

attention a decoration was awarded; it was called the Highly Derogatory Order of the Irremovable Digit.

Before he embarked on his humorous writing for Punch Willis had been the author of several historical novels. He was, however, to exchange this graver work for the production of light and amusing books and of crime stories which were also published in the United States. He produced, indeed, a bright and varied selection, which included many happily chosen themes. In his work for Punch he pursued the well-known vein of Punch prose and had soon learned to take up a casual, natural stance before his subjects. Later it was to stand him in good stead. He had been the creator of Private Pullthrough and other well-known military characters, and a number of volumes of humorous articles such as Warriors at Ease, Percival at Play, Britisher of Broadway, Warriors Paraded and Nothing to do with the War came to bear witness to his facility and pleasing wit. He could be fresh and unforced and his touch was delicately light. There was also on occasion much of the vivid and entertaining letter writer in his work. One of his happiest efforts was Taxi (1931) – the first book of the taxicab. It was full of information and written throughout with good sense and humour. Village at War (1941) completed an entertaining trilogy of which Cottage in the Country and We Like the Country were the earlier parts.

He was an irrepressible writer and right into old age was hard at it producing books, plays and radio scripts year by year skilfully adapting his gifts to the demands of the times. Late in life he was involved in a television gardening programme.

Anthony Armstrong wrote a number of plays. In 1929 The Repertory Theatre put on his Caught, a light and festive entertainment which was seen again at the Embassy Theatre. In 1932 he collaborated with Ian Hay in Orders are Orders and his own Ten Minute Alibi and Without Witness were played in 1933, again at the Embassy Theatre. The former concerned an exciting and ingenious murder and was seen a second time at the Comedy Theatre in 1935. The latter, on a somewhat similar theme, was less well sustained; but a year afterwards a revised version was put on at the Duke of York's Theatre. Sitting on a Fence, a "three door farce" was produced in 1935 at the Duchess

Theatre, and Mile Away Murder, another crime mystery, at the Westminster Theatre in 1937. He collaborated with Arnold Ridley in The Running Man (1949) and Bellamy (1959), and wrote several popular radio plays including For Love of a Lady, The Black King, Death Set to Music and The Wide Guy which was also made into a film.

He married, in 1926, Monica, only daughter of Dr A.L.M. Sealey. They had one son and two daughters.

Note:

The Strange Case of Mr. Pelham is curiously absent from an obituary that concentrates heavily on Anthony Armstrong's early writings as a humourist, playwright and editor. After this detailed attention there are only a few erratic updates for the second half of his career, with the last perfunctory revision appearing to be in the late 1950s. In doing so, the obituary misses several notable highlights, such as the films Orders are Orders (starring Peter Sellers, Sid James and Tony Hancock) and The Man Who Haunted Himself with Roger Moore. There is no mention Alfred Hitchcock's adaptation of The Strange Case of Mr. Pelham for a first-series episode of Alfred Hitchcock Presents in 1955. Neither are there mentions of important novels, such as the early five-volume series of Jimmie Rezaire private detective stories, or the later Spies in Amber, He Was Found in the Road or One Jump Ahead. It contains several factual slips: Armstrong's Country House series is a quintet and not a trilogy, the first volume of which is Cottage into House and not 'Cottage in the Country'. The play referred to as 'Caught' is presumably the 'Criminal Comedy in Three Acts' Well Caught.

Also Available from B7 Media

BOOKS

Marriage Bureau
Mary Oliver and Mary Benedetta
Additional material by Richard Kurti

AUDIOBOOKS

Bad Seed
By Richard Lieberman
Narrated by Sarah Borges

The Afterlives of Doctor Gachet
By Sam Meekings
Narrated by Sam Devereaux

The Strange Case of Mr. Pelham
By Anthony Armstrong
Narrated by Barnaby Eaton-Jones

Ray's Game
Written and read by Jools Berry

The Inspector Ryga Mysteries: Death in the Cove
By Pauline Rowson
Narrated by Jonathan Rhodes

The Inspector Ryga Mysteries: Death in the Harbour
By Pauline Rowson
Narrated by Jonathan Rhodes

BIOGRAPHIES

Comic Book Babylon
A Cautionary Tale of Sex, Drugs & Comics
Written and read by Tim Pilcher

In the Nick of Time
The Autobiography of John Altman
Written and read by John Altman

Marriage Bureau
By Mary Oliver and Mary Benedetta
Narrated by Helen Quigley

Roger Federer: Portrait of an Artist
By Sam Meekings
Narrated by Simon Johns

AUDIO DRAMAS

Dan Dare: The Audio Adventures
Based on the *Eagle* comic strip "Dan Dare"
created by Rev. Marcus Morris and Frank Hampson
Dramatised for audio by Richard Kurti, Bev Doyle, James Swallow,
Simon Guerrier, Patrick Chapman and Colin Brake
Starring Ed Stoppard, Geoff McGivern, Heida Reed, Michael Cochrane
and Raad Rawi as the Mekon

The Martian Chronicles
Based on the novel by Ray Bradbury
Dramatised for audio by Richard Kurti & Bev Doyle
Starring Derek Jacobi, Hayley Atwell, John Altman and Zoë Tapper

Eleanor of Aquitaine: Mother of the Pride
A play by Catherine Muschamp
Performed by Eileen Page

Acknowledgements

Thanks to Barnaby Eaton-Jones for his tireless shepherding of the project. Kenton Hall for his layout skills. Rob Hammond for the cover art. Jack Bowman, who went there and back again, to join all the dots. Sercha Cronin at Eric Glass. And, of course, Anthony Armstrong's grandson Jonathan Maas for entrusting B7 Media with the opportunity to republish and reintroduce Armstrong's iconic novel *The Strange Case of Mr. Pelham* to a new readership.

CPSIA information can be obtained
at www.ICGtesting.com
Printed in the USA
LVHW100724221221
706813LV00002B/26